Return to Flint

Return to Flint

Treasure Hernandez

www.urbanbooks.net

Urban Books, LLC
300 Farmingdale Road, NY-Route 109
Farmingdale, NY 11735

ISBN 13: 978-1-62286-477-5
ISBN 10: 1-62286-477-8

First Trade Paperback Printing April 2017
Printed in the United States of America

10 9 8 7 6 5 4 3 2 1

This is a work of fiction. Any references or similarities to actual events, real people, living or dead, or to real locales are intended to give the novel a sense of reality. Any similarity in other names, characters, places, and incidents is entirely coincidental.

Distributed by Kensington Publishing Corp.
Submit Orders to:
Customer Service
400 Hahn Road
Westminster, MD 21157-4627
Phone: 1-800-733-3000
Fax: 1-800-659-2436

Return to Flint

by

Treasure Hernandez

Chapter 1

The ticking sound of the large clock hanging on the wall to her left seemed inexplicably loud in Tiana's ears. Tick. Tock. Tick. Tock. The drab gray paint on the walls and the caged windows reminded her of where she was, although she didn't need reminding. Sweat dripped off the tip of her nose in cadence with the sound of the clock and the thump of her heartbeat. She shook all over, and her vision was becoming blurry with every minute she stayed in that familiar position.

Tiana moaned, a little trick she'd learned to keep herself conscious in times like these. She rocked a little, consciousness becoming harder to hold on to. Little squirms of light flashed through her eyes, and she had to concentrate to make herself blink them away. Tiana knew those came right before she usually succumbed to the drugs. She had been through this so many times she felt like a drug side effects expert. *If you blink and moan and force yourself to move any muscle on your body the medicine won't overcome you,* she told herself.

She moaned again, painfully aware of the throbbing in her scalp, the result of Dr. Syed's tight grasp on a fistful of her hair. He grunted lustfully, clamping down harder on her hair with one hand and using the other to unzip his pants. Tiana's head felt wavier than it had ever in the past. It had to be the new medication she had been forced to ingest a few minutes earlier.

The smell of Dr. Syed's dick caused the acids in Tiana's stomach to bubble up into the back of her throat. She didn't know how long she could take the strong odor. A mixture of musty body, dirty feet, and cheap men's cologne was what it smelled like to her. Tiana knew the scent on his dick meant she wasn't Dr. Syed's first victim of the day; he usually averaged three or four per day. If she opened her mouth, she'd taste the body fluids of the other girls. If she didn't, she'd be lying in her own body fluids for days. Thinking about it made her mentally and physically sick.

Forcing herself to swallow caused Tiana's head to spin a little bit. If she gagged, she would be punished more harshly than ever before. At least, that was the threat she got when she was dragged into the office kicking and fighting.

"C'mon, Caldoron, open up. Don't make this worse than it has to be. Be a good girl and get it hard. Lick it like you do." Dr. Syed panted lasciviously with a wicked smile on his face. He swiped the head of his flaccid, uncircumcised dick across Tiana's tightly clenched lips like it was the tip of a lipstick.

The feeling of the moist, clammy skin on her mouth caused another swirl of nausea to invade her stomach; this time, Tiana locked her jaw tighter in response. Her entire body felt hot like she had a fever, and she could feel a bitter swell of tears welling up in the backs of her eyes. Darkness had tried to creep up on her several times, but she fought the effects of the medication by moaning and blinking. Dr. Syed lifted his limp noodle and beat it on Tiana's lips this time, his sick attempt to get her to capitulate.

"Open your fucking mouth," he whispered through labored breaths.

Tiana still refused to open her mouth. She also refused to let her tears fall. Dr. Syed's abuse had become so regular now Tiana had conditioned herself to go numb. Tiana had been practicing how to fight against the effects of the medication he always forced on her, too, a skill that had proven more valuable than anything else she had learned during her time at the juvenile psychiatric hospital.

It's mind over matter. Mind over matter, Tiana chanted to herself. *Mind over . . .* Her thoughts kept slipping away. Her knees burned from being on them for so long, and her neck ached from the position Dr. Syed had her head held in.

"I said open your fucking mouth, you little bitch! Don't act like you don't enjoy our time together," he hissed, forcing her face farther into his musty crotch. "Open your fucking mouth, I said." Frustration and lust laced his words.

Tiana grunted as her body jerked forward from the force of his shove and caused her face to scrape against Dr. Syed's coarse pubic hairs. More vomit came into her mouth, but she just swallowed the acidic body fluid back down because letting it out would've meant opening her mouth.

"If you don't open your mouth you can guarantee a trip to the fucking padded room," Dr. Syed said through gritted teeth, "and this time you'll be there two weeks instead of two days." Dr. Syed wasn't used to this level of resistance from any of the girls.

Thinking about lying in that all-white padded room, bound by a straitjacket, left with no food or water for days, left to sit in her own piss and shit for days, and having those glaring, heated lights shining down on her prompted Tiana to open her mouth.

Dr. Syed smiled. "Attagirl," he said softly, pulling her head toward his now halfway five-inch dick. "Show me like you did last time." He closed his eyes, waiting to feel Tiana's warm mouth on him.

A single tear escaped out of the side of each of Tiana's eyes. They weren't the involuntary ones that came from the medicine loosening the tear ducts. These tears came from the hot ball of fury sizzling inside of her.

Tiana inhaled, closed her eyes and, with the quickness of a bear claw trap, she turned her head to the left and snapped her teeth down on the tip of Dr. Syed's dick. She bit down so hard sharp lightning bolts of pain traveled from her locked jaws up to the center of her head.

"Agh!" Dr. Syed shrieked. "Ah! Let me go! Let me go!"

Tiana released the grip on his dick and turned her head so she could get a mouthful of his inner left thigh. She continued to clamp down with the force of a great white shark. Fueled by Dr. Syed's cries for mercy, Tiana ground her teeth into the thick muscle of his thigh until she tasted the sharp, metallic sting of his blood on her tongue. She finally let go of his thigh, stood up, and ran to his desk. She opened the top left drawer, took out his phone, and started taking a video of what was going on.

"Yeah, you ain't so tough now, huh, Dr. Syed? It's not so much fun when the tip of your dick almost gets bitten off," Tatiana yelled at him while his blood dripped down her chin.

Dr. Syed was on the floor doubled over in pain. He was holding on to his penis in tears and hyperventilating from the throbbing sensation coming from the tip of his member.

"Now, why don't you tell your loving wife how you ended up getting hurt, Dr. Syed?" Tiana pointed the phone camera at him so his entire ordeal could be captured on video. "Tell her how you had me sucking your dick and I bit it."

"Arg! Tatiana." Dr. Syed tried to speak in between breaths. "Stop."

"Stop what, Dr. Syed? Stop recording you?" Tatiana bent over and got in his face. She turned the camera around so it could keep taking video of him and her. "You didn't stop when Elizabeth was crying and begging for you to stop raping her because she was bleeding and swollen. You didn't stop when Celeste was screaming out in pain the first time you butt-fucked her. No, this shit ain't gonna stop, Dr. Syed. Matter of fact, this is just the beginning for you, because I'm gonna upload this video to WorldStarHipHop so everyone can see you for the monster you really are."

Dr. Syed started taking deep breaths to calm himself down. He was able to get his breathing under control, and he slowly made his way back onto the couch. While he did that, Tiana gave his full name in the video, where he worked, and very vivid details of the things that he had been doing to Tiana and her two friends at William P. Rollins Psychiatric Hospital in central Michigan.

"Tatiana," he began to reason with her, "put the phone down. You don't want to do that."

"Fuck yeah, I do. I want the world to know about the sick shit that you been up to. God knows how many other girls you've taken advantage of over the years. I'm gonna upload this to YouTube, too. They'll take it down once they see your ugly naked ass, but enough people will see it by then, and I'm sure the cops will come to arrest you and your life will be over," Tatiana said confidently. It felt good to be able to stand up to this man after months and months of torture from him and his staff.

"Okay, okay, what will it take for you to delete this video and put tonight behind us?" Dr. Syed questioned.

Tiana broke out the biggest smile. This was going exactly like she'd hoped it would. "You're going to release me, Celeste, and Elizabeth as soon as possible. You're also going to give me five thousand dollars cash and have a car come and pick us up from here and take us to the Courtyard Flint Grand Blanc on Gateway Centre."

"Done. It's going to take a few days for me to process the paperwork for your release, but I will make all of the arrangements in the meantime," Dr. Syed agreed. He didn't have any real plans to do anything she asked of him. He figured that for now, he'd tell her everything she wanted to hear so she could delete the video. He wondered if Tatiana had heard a word he'd said because she seemed really engrossed in whatever she was doing on his phone.

"Well, just in case you decide to go back on everything you just agreed to, I e-mailed this video to a friend of mine who will be waiting for me to see her when I'm out of here. I told her if she doesn't see me in two weeks on the outside to go ahead and release the video for me," Tatiana said with a satisfied smirk on her face.

"You have my word. I will put in the paperwork tomorrow, and you and the girls should be out of here in no more than four days," Dr. Syed reassured her. He was mad that she had been smart enough to send out the video to a third party. Now he had no choice but to comply with her demands. He was a little bummed that his three favorite patients would soon be leaving him, but he knew he'd quickly find other girls to replace them. His main concern now was tending to his still-bleeding thigh and injured penis. He had no idea how he was going to explain it to his wife.

Tatiana threw the phone at him and went to the sink to clean the blood off of her face. She couldn't wait to get back to her room so she could tell the girls they were going to be released in four days.

Four Days Later

"Yo, Tiana, you sleeping or what?" Cee Cee whispered, elbowing Tiana in the ribs. "Wake up. Wake up."

Tiana blinked rapidly and shook her head a little bit, trying to get rid of the nightmare she'd been dreaming about. She touched her face, making sure that her lip wasn't still swollen from biting Dr. Syed a few days ago. She hadn't realized that night that when she bit down on him, she had injured her lip as well. Her lip had been puffy and swollen the last couple of days.

"You okay, boo?" Cee Cee asked her with a concerned expression on her face.

"Yeah, I'm okay. I was just having a bad dream."

"Okay, good. Wake up, bitch! Today is the day!" Cee Cee jumped on the bed and started shaking Tatiana. "We're getting out this motherfucker!"

Tatiana was happy to see how excited her friend was. It was nice to see Cee Cee smiling and happy.

The grumpy CNA who worked the morning shift walked into their room. "Caldoron and Sorrentino. Congratulations. You get to go home today," she said with no enthusiasm in her voice whatsoever. "Come with me to go over the final paperwork, and then you are free to go."

The two girls exchanged looks. Neither of them could believe that the day had finally come.

They were escorted down to the front desk and taken into a side office, where they signed some release forms. Fifteen minutes later they walked out of the two front doors into the cool, crisp autumn air. Tatiana looked around for a black van that was supposed to be picking them up to take them to the hotel, but she didn't see anyone. Then she remembered the front desk receptionist had given her an envelope that she said was for her from Dr. Syed. She pulled it out of her back pocket and looked to see what was in it.

Inside was only $2,000 cash and a note that said a car would be waiting for them at a nearby gas station to take them to a motel on Dort Highway. Tatiana was pissed to see that Dr. Syed had only given her $2,000, but she wasn't about to go back in and wait for his shift to start to confront him about it. She had plans for him so she figured he'd get what was coming to him.

The girls walked down to the gas station and, sure enough, there was a white Caravan waiting for them. They hopped in, and they both looked behind them to see the building that had given them so many nightmares get smaller and smaller as the car took them farther down the long road that would take them to their future.

"Cee Cee, I have an idea," Tatiana whispered to her so the driver couldn't hear what she was going to say.

"What is it?" Cee Cee asked.

"How about, instead of waiting, we just get Dr. Syed's ass right now?"

"Right now?" Cee Cee's eyes became wide. "How?" was all she wanted to know.

"You know where Izzy is staying at, right?"

"Yeah. That's the motel we're heading to right now," Cee Cee replied.

For whatever reason, Elizabeth had gotten released one day before them. Tatiana had been at a group meeting when Izzy was released, so Elizabeth spoke to Celeste. Instead of going straight to the Courtyard, Izzy agreed to stay the night at a motel and wait for them there so that they could head out to the hotel together.

"Okay, I'm gonna see if I can get the driver to let me borrow his phone so we can call Elizabeth at the motel she's staying at. I'm going to have Elizabeth give me all the information she has on Dr. Syed so we can track down where he lives."

"You want us to go to his house?" Cee Cee asked, trying to figure out where Tiana was going with this plan of hers.

"Yes!"

"And what are we gonna do at his house? Knock on his door and try to sell him and his wife some Girl Scout Cookies?" Cee Cee asked.

"Nope," Tatiana replied completely unfazed by Cee Cee's sarcasm. "We are going to go to his house and blow his shit up!" Tiana said excitedly while she kept her voice at a whisper. "But, first, we have to pick up some dark clothes; and then I need to get to AutoZone to pick up some knickknacks."

Chapter 2

"Tiana, my legs are cramping up," Cee Cee complained.

Tiana whipped her head around to see Cee Cee bouncing up and down with her legs bent at the knees. "Hold on, Cee Cee," Tiana whispered back, getting her bearings. "I'm cramping up too. My back is killing me from crouching down like this. This nigga taking mad long to come out, though. I'm sick of waiting, for real."

"I know. My nerves got me fucked up. I gotta use the bathroom, too," Cee Cee confessed.

"We are troopers. We don't get nervous about shit, and we will wait for days if we have to," Tiana said.

Cee Cee nodded in agreement. "What you say is all good, but my fucking legs are burning crouching down over here for all of these hours. I don't think I'm gonna be able to walk straight after this," Celeste joked.

"You ain't never lie." Tiana chuckled.

It was early morning, and the sun was coming up in Dr. Syed's neighborhood as the area came alive with people. Tiana and Cee Cee were getting nervous that someone would spot them crouched down in the shrubbery between Dr. Syed's house and his neighbor's house. The expansive backyards of the estates gave the girls some cover, but they knew if they got spotted it would be all over for them. It was bad enough Tiana and Cee Cee looked like two burglars dressed in all black; all it would take was one nosy neighbor and their cover would be blown.

Another hour passed before they saw any movement in front of Dr. Syed's house. Cee Cee was the first one to notice. "Look," Celeste whispered, urging Tiana back up onto her knees. "Do you see what the fuck I'm seeing?"

"That's that nigga right now," Tiana said, getting ready to smile.

"Yeah, but look," Cee Cee said, her words breaking off.

Tiana's smile never got to form on her lips; instead, her jaw dropped slightly and her brows furrowed. Tiana's and Cee Cee's bodies stiffened and their breath caught in their throats. Tiana swallowed hard, and Cee Cee's eyes went as round as saucers. For a few seconds, neither of them said anything; they just stared at what was unfolding in front of them.

"He's not by himself," Cee Cee said, panic strung through her words.

"I can fucking see that," Tiana snapped, her lips turning white while her heart hammered against her chest bone.

"I thought you said he didn't have any kids. You said it was just a wife," Celeste spat. "Tiana, we gotta stop this from going down. I ain't sign up for this shit right here. Nah, we gotta stop it," Cee Cee demanded, her voice forceful but shaky. "We can't go through with it. Not now. Not like this."

"Are you kidding me? What the fuck we going to do, Cee Cee? Run out there and say, 'Yo, Dr. Syed, don't get in your car because we rigged that shit with dynamite'?" Tiana said, glaring at Celeste. "There is nothing we can do now. Izzy said when she got into his office that she didn't see no evidence that this nigga had kids, but now we see she was wrong. What the fuck we going to do now? Nothing, that's what. We here, the trap is laid, and we can't turn back or else everything we've been planning for is over. Our lives will be fucking over, Cee Cee. It's either us or him," Tiana whispered harshly, getting close to Cee Cee's face so that Cee Cee could hear her loud and clear.

"You're wrong, Tiana. We can go out there and stop it. We can't let an innocent kid just die like that, Tiana. So, Izzy made a fucking mistake. It's up to us now to fix this shit," Celeste whispered back just as harshly, putting her feet flat on the dirt and preparing to rise on her legs.

Tiana snatched Cee Cee by her hoodie and pulled her back down into the thick bushes behind Dr. Syed's house. Cee Cee landed on her butt with a thud. Tiana wasted no time getting in her face.

"Cee Cee, you can't be that fucking weak. I know you come from a rich family and you're used to having shit laid out for you and all that bullshit, but you have to be smarter than this. You think this shit is just that easy? Just as hard as it was to plan, it's even harder to stop it now. We didn't just plan to blow some random nigga up. This is the fucking devil. This the nigga who did unthinkable shit to us who we talking about here. What the hell? You act like you can't fucking remember. Think about all the shit he did and then went home at night like he ain't do nothing. Think about the fucking abortion he had performed on you with no pain medication or anesthesia, how you bled like a stuck pig for three weeks and the nigga was still making you suck his dick because he couldn't fuck you. Think about Izzy and all the times that nigga fucked her raw until she couldn't walk the next day and how she would be in such shock she would barely talk to us or eat or sleep," Tiana said through gritted teeth, fisting Cee Cee's hoodie so tight her knuckles throbbed. Tiana's head swirled from a rush of adrenaline.

"You can't feel sorry for a piece of shit like him, Cee Cee. He didn't give a fuck about you and still doesn't," Tiana preached. In her rundown to Cee Cee, Tiana didn't use herself as an example because talking about the things Dr. Syed did to her was way too painful for her.

"I know all of that, okay? But, this ain't right. It ain't right," Cee Cee said, a hot stream of tears suddenly falling from her face. "It's a little kid. A fucking little kid," she cried, folding her arms across her body, hugging herself.

Tiana sighed and shook her head. She couldn't even look at her friend right then. Tiana hated when the other girls showed any weakness because it reminded her of just how coldhearted she had become inside.

"I know Dr. Syed deserves to die. I'm down for that, but to kill a kid is a sin. It's a sin, and the karma will come back on us like some shit we can't handle," Celeste continued to press.

Tiana sucked her teeth in disgust. She always knew Cee Cee was a softy, but she hadn't expected her to break down like this. Now, listening to Cee Cee whimpering like a baby, she realized she should have done this shit by herself. It was a bad idea to drag Cee Cee into this. Not everybody was cut out for this type of lifestyle, and Tiana knew it. It was one thing to talk about killing somebody, and it was another thing to actually go through with it. Tiana was painfully aware that she was the more heartless of the two of them. She had never been one for much crying and feeling sorry for people. This pampered princess role Cee Cee was putting on was getting Tiana annoyed.

"You can cry for that sick nigga if you want to. What's done is done. The kid is just going to have to be a casualty of war. Fuck it, life ain't always fair," Tiana said flatly, her words devoid of any remorse. Tiana had learned from her father to be swift with her actions and to say what you mean and mean what you say. Her father had taught her from a young age that the best way to execute a plan is to detach yourself emotionally from it. It was a skill that took some getting used to, but once you mastered it, plans were a lot easier to follow through with.

"I'm not going to let you fuck this up for us, Cee Cee. I love you and the whole nine yards, but this shit is going down. If you can't stomach it then don't watch," Tiana said, turning her face away from Celeste.

Celeste slumped to the ground and turned her body so she couldn't see the front of Dr. Syed's house any longer. She put her hands over her ears in an attempt to drown out the sound of the little boy's laughter.

Tiana knew what they were about to do was tearing Celeste up inside, but Tiana also knew they had no choice now. Still, Tiana didn't want Celeste to be mad at her. Truthfully, Celeste and Izzy were the closest thing to family she had right now. Her father was killed almost two years ago, and her mother had died from complications when she was born. Technically, she still had her stepmother; but, being that she had ended up in that mental institution because of her, she wasn't exactly on her "people I can trust" list. She hadn't been looking to make friends when she met Celeste and Elizabeth in the psych ward, but now that she had them, she didn't want to let them go.

Tiana softened her facial expression and her tone. "Cee Cee, it's his fault this shit had to happen," Tiana said softly, giving Cee Cee's shoulder a comforting squeeze. "He did some unforgivable shit to us. We didn't know a kid would be here; but if we go back on it now, we will end up locked up again, and then he will do some cruel, animalistic shit to us," Tiana reminded Cee Cee.

Cee Cee shook her head in agreement, but she still didn't turn back around to watch.

Tiana turned her attention back to watching Dr. Syed and the little boy. The nervousness she had felt when she first saw the little boy had faded into a burning, vengeful hatred. Kid or no kid, Dr. Syed had to die for everything that he'd done to Tiana, Cee Cee, and Izzy. Suddenly,

Izzy's pretty face flashed through Tiana's mind and her anxiousness to get the deed done increased. Tiana's chest heaved up and down now.

Get in the fucking car. Get in the fucking car, Tiana chanted in her head, her fists clenched tightly. She was so close to exacting revenge that she could feel every nerve in her body coming alive.

Tiana watched Dr. Syed through squinted eyes as he threw his head back and laughed out loud. Even from a distance, his laugh sent chills down her spine. *What man who is a father would do the things he did to us? A sick bastard like him doesn't deserve a child.*

The little boy seemed happier than a kid in a candy store as he ran from Dr. Syed while they played tag. He giggled and looked behind him as he ran around baiting Dr. Syed to catch him.

"Got you!" Dr. Syed called out playfully, grabbing the boy in a playful football hold. This was definitely a different side of the perverted doctor from what Tiana was used to seeing. She clenched her fists, infuriated at the sight.

Dr. Syed bounced the boy as he carried him, giggling and kicking his legs, to the back seat of a midnight blue Range Rover. It was the car that Izzy had told the girls belonged to Dr. Syed. Seemed more like a drug dealer's ride, Tiana had thought weeks ago when Izzy first told them about the car as they sat in their room eating lunch.

For whatever reason, Dr. Syed had taken Izzy out of the facility and brought her with him when he stepped out to grab breakfast. Of course, Dr. Syed didn't have her ride in the car for the sheer purpose of taking Izzy out to get some fresh air. He made her suck him off on the way over to the store, and he fingered her all the way back until they pulled into the parking lot. The front desk girls commended him for being such a thoughtful doctor and going the extra mile for his patients. Little did they know the monster he really was.

Tiana's heart thudded up in her chest now as she moved from her knees onto her tiptoes, the anticipation of what was coming causing her legs to shake fiercely.

"He's getting in the fucking car, Cee Cee. He's getting in the fucking car," Tiana whispered almost breathlessly, her legs trembling now.

Cee Cee closed her eyes tightly and shook her head from left to right and started to mouth a prayer; but before she could complete one sentence, boom!

Her body was thrust back as if she had been pushed forcefully, and she involuntarily inhaled a mouthful of dirt. "Oh my God!" Cee Cee coughed out, her ears ringing from the loud blast.

The force of the blast had sent Tiana flying backward, and she had landed flat on her back a few steps away from her friend. "Ouch." Tiana winced, covering her ringing ears with her hands and rocking back and forth. Dirt covered her face and made her eyes feel like someone had poured fine grains of sand into them. The back of her head felt like she'd been hit with a sledgehammer, but she still had their escape plan at the forefront of her mind.

"Cee Cee?" Tiana croaked, struggling to open her eyes. "Sss." Tiana cringed, suddenly feeling a small trickle of blood near her right eye.

"Mmm," Cee Cee moaned, struggling to lift herself up from the ground.

Celeste's chin was bleeding, and she had a few scrapes on her hands.

Tiana's hearing was impaired, and her back ached like she'd been stomped out. "We gotta go, Cee Cee. C'mon. The cops and the bomb squad will be here any minute," Tiana panted, struggling to her feet and grabbing on to her friend.

"Is it done?" Celeste asked, seemingly disoriented from the blast. "Tiana! Is the little boy dead?" Celeste screamed out.

Tiana quickly and roughly forced her hand over Celeste's mouth, pulling her back down behind the bushes. "Shhh!"

"Mmm! Mmm!" Cee Cee moaned through the skin of Tiana's hand. "Mmm. Wmmww." Celeste kept making noise.

Tiana could tell Cee Cee was still demanding to know if the boy was dead. Tiana clutched her friend tightly in a bear hug. It was a method that had worked numerous times while they were locked up in the psychiatric hospital together. "Shhh."

Cee Cee melted against Tiana and sobbed.

"Shhh. It was either him or us, Cee Cee. Him or us. Remember our pact. We are the abused ones, and we were gonna get him back for what he did to us. Him or us. We kill him first," Tiana comforted her.

"Him or us. We kill him first," Cee Cee repeated after her.

Chapter 3

Cee Cee stopped running, bent over, and put her hands on her knees, trying to catch her breath. Tiana was just a few feet ahead of her. Tiana's long, slender legs and past track experience gave her a slight advantage.

"C'mon, we're almost there," Tiana huffed, whipping her head around to make sure no one had seen them running away from the crime scene.

It had taken no time for what seemed like the entire police department, fire department, and any other specialized team to respond to the explosion. Tiana and Cee Cee had heard the wail of numerous sirens as they cut through houses, backyards, and small patches of forests during their escape. Now they walked along the highway just out of the sight of cars and passersby.

"Cee Cee, I'm pretty sure this is the motel Izzy is supposed to be waiting for us at," Tiana said, her words coming out like puffs of air. They had stopped running and started walking now since they were close to the planned destination. "We just have to go to the front desk and ask for her. Do you remember the name she said she gave them?" Tiana asked her.

"Yeah, I do." Celeste chuckled a little bit. "Bonita Applebottom." Both girls busted out laughing when Cee Cee said the name out loud. "I swear, Izzy be bugging out sometimes."

"Yeah, she's crazy," Tiana agreed. "Let's go inside. You do the talking."

The girls walked into a room not much bigger than a closet. There was an old, torn, worn-out chair with doo-doo brown pleather on it. In front of it was a beat-up old wooden desk that looked like it was standing on its last good leg. An old man who looked to be in his late sixties with crusty, dirty black-and-white hair sat behind the desk, smoking a cigar.

"Can I help you?" he asked with an attitude.

"Yes, hi, we're supposed to be meeting our friend. I believe she has a room here." Cee Cee paused and waited for the old man to ask her for the name.

Instead, he just puffed on his cigar and looked at her like she had two heads. "Little girl, do I look like the type who gives enough fucks to take guest names down?" He began to chuckle as if he'd told a funny joke, but his chuckle quickly turned into a dry, nasty cough. "What she look like?" he asked.

"She has long black hair, her eyes are kinda chinky, and she has light brown skin." Cee Cee tried her best to describe what their friend looked like. She couldn't wait to get out of that stuffy little room.

"Oh, I know who you talking about. That hot little cute thang with the wide hips and small titties. She been here since two days ago. She's in room twenty-three," he informed them.

"Okay, thank you, mister." Cee Cee and Tiana quickly turned and made their way toward the door.

"Hey, I have a proposition for you two pretty young thangs," the old man said just as Tiana was about to push the door open.

The girls turned their heads slightly to hear what he had to say.

"How about you two have a little fun with old Charlie here and I'll let y'all and your friend stay two extra nights for free," he said as he grabbed his crotch and licked his lips to expose a mouthful of missing teeth.

"We'll pass, thank you," Tiana said in a flat tone. With that being said, she and Cee Cee walked out of the office and followed the signs that told them what order the rooms were in. They made their way to room twenty-three, and Cee Cee knocked gently on the door. Within seconds, Izzy was at the door and let them in.

"Damn, Izzy, you didn't even bother to ask who it was," Tiana said as she walked past her.

"I didn't have to. I knew it was you two," Izzy replied.

"No, you didn't," Tiana snapped at her. "You assumed it was us. It could have been the cops or anybody else knocking on that door."

"No, it couldn't have, because nobody else knows I'm staying here," Izzy argued back.

"Tiana, give it a rest. You don't always have to be so serious about everything," Cee Cee interjected. "Just try to relax for a minute. We're finally out of that hellhole, and we can try to get our lives together."

"Yeah, we're out, but we still have shit that needs to be taken care of."

"Speaking of taking care of shit, how'd it go with Dr. Syed? Is he dead yet?" Izzy asked.

Cee Cee took a deep breath and explained to Izzy how things had gone down with Dr. Syed and his kid.

"Damn, that's messed up," Izzy said, full of remorse. She would have never wanted for a kid to lose his life in the process of them getting their revenge on Dr. Syed. It wasn't the kid's fault his father was a sick and depraved rapist.

"Yeah, it's messed up, but there was nothing we could do about it," Tiana tried to reason with them. The three girls sat solemnly on the beds.

After a few minutes, Tiana decided to break up the negative vibe in the room. "Okay, so we're going to stick to plan B just like we decided," Tiana said, breaking the silence. "We're going to spend one night together in this motel to try to get some sleep. Then we're going to head out and go our separate ways. We have to lie low until shit dies down about Dr. Syed's death."

"You don't have to remind me. I know the plan. You just can't wait to get back to your old life and have us split up, huh?" Cee Cee spoke with attitude and resentment in her voice. She stood up from the bed and made her way toward the bathroom.

Tiana stopped her midstride, grabbing Cee Cee by the shoulder and spinning her around so they were facing each other. "I know this shit wasn't perfect, but I will never forget you or Izzy. I'm not looking forward to us splitting up right now, but it's what we have to do. You two are my best friends now, and I consider y'all my sisters." Tiana looked straight into Cee Cee's eyes as she spoke. "I hope y'all feel the same way about me. Remember: since the first day we ever talked to each other in there, all we had was each other," Tiana said with feeling.

Celeste stared at her in silence for a few seconds, and Tiana stared back, their eyes glinting with the pain of where they'd been and what they'd gone through. Just like that, Tiana was thrust back to when they first met.

William P. Rollins Psychiatric Hospital
One Year and Two Months Earlier

"Get off of me! Get the fuck off of me!" Tiana screamed, dropping herself to the floor, kicking, and flailing her arms. "I'm not supposed to be here! Get off me!" Tiana flailed so wildly that the white gauze wrapped around both of her wrists immediately became soaked through

with blood. She had busted the stitches on her wrist wounds.

"Arrgh!" Tiana growled, trying to bite one of the men holding her down.

"We need sedation! Somebody get a fucking needle over here!" a tall, skinny hospital orderly barked just before one of Tiana's wild kicks landed right in his crotch.

"Ouch! This little bitch," the orderly shrieked, releasing his grasp on Tiana and falling to his knees.

Tiana took the opportunity to kick him again, but she wasn't able to get a third kick in before at least ten men rained down on her. Tiana felt hands all over her body, and they weren't gentle touches, either.

"No! No! Get off me!" Tiana squealed so hard and loud the back of her throat burned. When it was all said and done, it had taken twelve orderlies and two security guards to get her into a position where they could stick her with the needle filled with Ativan.

Tiana had tried screaming from the pain of the needle prick, but the medicine took effect so quickly her mouth just hung open with no sound coming out of it.

Tiana's body relaxed within a few seconds, and her head lolled to the side. She could hear footsteps around her and see light, but she couldn't react or control her body movements.

"Ready? One, two, three, up." The orderlies' voices sounded robotic in Tiana's ears. She felt herself being hoisted up and then slammed down onto a stretcher. Tears drained out of the sides of her eyes, but not because she had made them come. She felt herself moving, but it felt more like she was floating.

Right before her eyes closed on their own, Tiana saw two girls huddled together watching everything that was happening to her. Both girls had looks of genuine concern and pity etched into their facial expressions. It was like they knew something that Tiana didn't know. Tiana didn't understand why they looked so concerned when they didn't even know her name.

Tiana spent three days in a straitjacket locked in an all-white padded room before she was let out to mix with the other patients on the floor.

"Let's go, Caldoron. I ain't got all day. Step lively or go back to the white room!" an orderly had screamed as Tiana shuffled her feet, trying to keep up with him. The odor emanating from her body was making Tiana herself sick. She hadn't had a shower since the police had picked her up from the local hospital where she had been treated for the deep self-inflicted cuts on her wrists.

Tiana felt like she had to learn to walk all over again and her body ached in places she didn't even know existed. She had been so drugged up, and tied down for so long, that it was as if her brain wasn't sending signals to the rest of her body parts. A few times she'd even stumbled, nearly spilling to the floor flat on her face. She was mad at her body for betraying her like that. If she hadn't been drugged up, she could've been trying to figure a way out of there.

"Here you go. This is your bed, and this is your side. Stay on your side and on your bed, and there won't be no problems. Got it?" the dark, lanky, bull-faced orderly told Tiana, dumping a blanket roll and a small hospital basin filled with toiletries onto a tiny, unmade metal-spring bed that had a thin stripped mattress atop it.

Tiana collapsed onto the bed and closed her eyes. Suddenly, before she could fight against it, a deep, comatose type of sleep overcame her and everything faded to black.

"Please, no! Please, not tonight! I'll do anything! Just don't take me!"

Tiana thought she was having anther nightmare when she was jerked out of her sleep to the sound of a high-pitched, squeaky, pleading voice. She had no idea how long she'd been asleep. Although it hurt Tiana's head to open her eyes, she did it anyway. Her eyes went round when she noticed two men dragging one of her roommates from her bed. Tiana sat up, her head throbbing. It quickly registered with her that the girl's face was familiar.

"What are y'all doing to her? Where y'all taking her?" Tiana croaked through cracked, dry lips. Her throat burned with every word and, even though she was trying to speak loudly, her voice barely came out above a whisper.

As one of the men walked by her, she tried to reach out to him and was able to pull at his pant leg. The man turned on Tiana and glared at her with the most evil blaze in his eyes. "Stay quiet, keep your hands to your fucking self, and mind your business before you get thrown back in the room," the man growled, baring his yellow teeth like a wild animal on the attack.

"Please! Please!" Tiana's roommate continued to cry as the men dragged her past Tiana's bed and out of the room.

Tiana struggled to her feet and rushed as fast as she could to the door, but her view and movements were obstructed right away by the broad body of one of the orderlies.

"Go back to bed, Caldoron. It's for your own fucking good," the Kimbo Slice look alike said, pushing Tiana in the chest and pulling the door to the room shut. At that time, Tiana didn't know how often she would be seeing the face of Daniel, the orderly, after that.

Tiana turned around in the darkness and began moving back toward her bed.

"Don't worry. You'll find out where they took her real soon and then you won't be so fast to want to know," said a voice in the darkness.

Tiana jumped; the eerie tone in the voice gave her chills. *"What? Who?"* Tiana squinted. The source of the voice moved closer to Tiana's bed. Through the darkness, she could see the silhouette of a petite girl with long, wavy hair.

"I'm Celeste," the voice said, boldly flopping down on the end of Tiana's bed. *"The girl they just dragged out of here is Elizabeth, but she likes to be called Izzy."*

Tiana looked at the girl tentatively. She didn't trust many people.

"When people introduce themselves you follow up by introducing yourself," Celeste told her. Celeste reached over and turned on the bedside lamp closest to Tiana's bed. She surveyed Tiana up and down and smiled like she knew a secret that Tiana didn't know.

Tiana raised her eyebrows at the personal intrusion. *"I'm Tatiana, but you can call me Tiana."*

"So I guess you're here for trying to commit suicide too?" Celeste said, nodding toward the old, dingy, bloodstained gauze pads on Tiana's wrists.

"Something like that," Tiana replied, looking at the nasty dried blood on the wrappings, then shuffling her hands so neither of them could see them anymore.

"Well, so did I and so did Izzy. That's why we are here too," Celeste said, her voice trailing off. *"I wasn't bold enough to do what you did, though. My death choice was pills and alcohol mixed with a big 'fuck you' to everybody I knew. I just took whatever I could find. I'm not into physical pain."*

"How long have you and Elizabeth been here?" Tiana asked with no sympathy in her voice for Celeste's suicide confession.

"We both got here the same week," Celeste replied, jumping up from Tiana's bed abruptly and returning to her own bed. "We've been here almost two months, but it feels like forever."

"Well, I'm planning on being here just a few more days. I'll be damned if they think they're going to keep me here more than a month."

"Yeah, we thought the same thing when we first got here. They're gonna keep you here as long as they want. You'll see. Good night, Tiana," Celeste said.

Tiana tried to keep the conversation going, but Celeste didn't say another word.

Tiana wasn't awake when Izzy was brought back to their room, but even in her dreams, Tiana could hear Izzy sobbing like her entire world had just ended. It wasn't until she got up the next day that she saw the blood droplets leading from the door to Izzy's bed.

"You what, Cee Cee? We don't need to rush to go our separate ways so fast." She smiled at her friend. "Tomorrow morning let's all grab some breakfast and then head to the Courtyard like we had originally wanted to do. We can hang out in the room, relax, and spend two nights together there. We still have some money from the two grand Dr. Syed gave us, so we'll be good."

"Really? That sounds amazing," Cee Cee said excitedly.

"That sounds great, Tiana," Izzy agreed. "I've never been to a fancy hotel like that," she admitted.

"All the more reason for us to go," Tiana stated. She felt good that she had managed to cheer up her two best friends, and she decided she'd make the best out of the next two days she'd get to spend with them.

Chapter 4

"This shit is not bad for two girls who broke out of a psychiatric hospital with nothing and no one to run to after offing their sick, twisted psychiatrist." Tiana beamed as she, Izzy, and Celeste entered their room at the Courtyard by Marriott. "Shit, Cee Cee, you're a genius for this one. Look how easy it was for you to say you were some doctor's daughter and get a room without showing some form of ID or anything. I swear, when you're in these high-society neighborhoods there ain't shit you can't get," Tiana asserted, rushing over to check out the wet bar.

"Tiana, you make it seem like you didn't grow up living comfortable too," Izzy pointed out.

"I never said I grew up starving in the ghetto. I grew up comfortable, but Cee Cee grew up a whole lot better than me," Tiana replied.

"It would've been even better if I'd had some Rag & Bone jeans, a Givenchy T-shirt, some Gucci stilettos, and a Céline bag waiting for my ass out here for when I got out. I'm so tired of looking like a fucking runaway refugee it's not even funny," Cee Cee griped in that perfect, pampered princess way that only she could pull off.

"We sure picked the right one to send to the front desk," Tiana mumbled and shook her head. "All your ass thinks about is clothes, shoes, and bags."

The girls had all decided that when they checked into the hotel, they would send Celeste to the front desk to check in because Celeste knew how to turn on the proper English and act like a pampered little rich girl who could simply use her eyes and facial expressions to dare a lowly front desk clerk to question her.

Tiana knew her strong alpha-type personality, her street swag, and that little hint of attitude that traced through all of her words would not have gone unnoticed, and the front desk clerk definitely would have requested identification from her before giving her a room.

Celeste was the right one for the job with her model poise, and beauty queen looks, too. Tiana always thought Celeste was the prettiest of them all. Celeste had perfectly straight white teeth, light brown almond-shaped eyes, and high cheekbones; and her blemish-free olive skin tone gave her that Kardashian family, Arabian princess type of glow. Celeste, who was half Haitian, half Italian, had what Tiana always referred to as that Italian princess body: big, perfect boobs, a flat stomach, slightly rounded hips, and a round, plump booty that looked like it was store-bought and chiseled by the surgery gods themselves. Her wavy dirty blond hair hung down to the middle of her back. At nineteen years old, Celeste managed to get a man's attention by just walking into a room.

Tiana, on the other hand, felt like she was the average Puerto Rican girl with light brown skin, a fairly cute face, and shoulder-length curly hair. Tiana was secretly jealous of Celeste's striking beauty. She would never hate on Cee Cee; she just hated feeling so average when she was around her friend.

Tiana failed to realize that she was beautiful in her own right. Tiana was always taller than most girls her age, standing five foot eight inches tall. She had an athletic, track star's body and was pretty tall considering she was full-blooded Puerto Rican. Most Puerto Rican females were of average height. Her breasts filled a 36C cup and were perfectly round and perky. She had four-pack abs, curvy hips with a small heart-shaped backside, and thick, toned thighs that looked amazing in skinny jeans or a short, tight dress. She had piercing brown eyes and full, pouty pink lips that stood out from her light brown complexion.

Her curly black hair framed her face in a way that gave her that exotic Latina flair. Since she had been locked in the hospital, Tiana kept her hair lazily combed out and unkempt. Her bangs hung over her face, giving her this crazy, deranged look. She walked with her head hung low, and she scared staff when they'd try to look into her face and see her brown eyes staring at them through the mess that was her hair. It was a far cry from how she looked out in the real world when she took care of herself. Compared to Celeste and Elizabeth, Tiana was the one who had scared the hospital staff and other patients the most. At twenty-four, she was the oldest of the three girls, and she had become very overprotective of them.

"I need a shower and a nap," Cee Cee huffed, kicking off her sneakers and unzipping her hoodie. All of the bending, ducking, and running in the past seventy-two hours had her aching all over. She may have had a nice body, but the only sport she'd ever indulged in was running through the stores at the mall. This was their only day at the hotel, and at the motel last night she hadn't felt like she had really been able to rest the way she had hoped she would.

"Yeah, I feel you. You can go to sleep. I'll be up. I want to watch the news and see if they're saying anything about the explosion. If they're suspecting it has any connections to his patients, we're going to have to leave here as soon as possible, Cee Cee. We'll just get a few winks, and then we gotta bounce," Tiana replied, shrugging out of her hoodie.

"Yeah, I know, I know," Celeste grumbled as she headed into the bathroom.

"Don't sound like that. We just did what we had to do," Tiana reaffirmed.

Celeste didn't respond, but the slamming door told Tiana that Celeste was still upset about killing the little boy. Tiana shook her head, cracked open an Absolut vodka nip, took it to the head, and then picked up the television remote and clicked it on.

"I knew this shit would be all over the news," Tiana whispered, finishing the tiny bottle of vodka and squinting at the television screen.

A reporter said, "Police and fire officials have confirmed that a prominent and much-respected psychiatrist, Dr. Peter Syed, died in an apparent car explosion outside of his home yesterday. Police have not confirmed this, but we are also told by a source that a child as young as four years old may have also been in the car when it exploded. Neighbors here say they are shocked. They speculate that the child may have been the doctor's nephew because the doctor did not have children of his own. Right now, police are not saying whether this explosion was the result of something faulty in the vehicle or whether they suspect foul play. Dr. Syed was head of the psychiatric evaluation department at William P. Rollins Psychiatric Hospital in Detroit. We will keep you updated on this very tragic event."

Tiana listened to the reporter's words, and waves of nausea rolled through her stomach. She didn't know if it was the excitement of knowing that she and the girls had pulled off a perfect hit—one that would've made her father proud—or if it was anxiety leaving her body knowing that they had been able to kill this bastard doctor who had abused, raped, and tormented her and the girls for so long.

Tiana was so transfixed by the news that she hadn't even heard Izzy enter the room. She had run down to the lobby to purchase bottles of water for them. "So I was right after all. He didn't have a kid," she said.

"Yeah, it wasn't his kid," Tiana replied.

At that moment Cee Cee came out of the bathroom. "So now they saying that the kid wasn't even his? We killed someone else's baby?" Cee Cee asked, her face folded into a scowl. "This is all types of fucked up, Tatiana."

"Look! Stop blaming me. We all planned this and it just so fucking happened to be the little boy was there. It's over and what's done is done," Tiana snapped as the knot of anger and anxiety in her chest finally unraveled. She hung her head as a quick pang of guilt came over her like a dark hood. She knew Cee Cee was mad because she called Tiana by her full name. She almost never did that.

"Blaming you? Believe it or not shit's not always about you," Cee Cee fired back.

Tiana quickly shook off the feeling of dread and guilt that had trampled on her mood. *Fuck it. What's done it done,* Tiana told herself. She could hear her father's voice in her head: *"When you have to kill somebody to protect yourself or your family there is nothing to feel guilty about."* He would've never approved of killing kids, but under the circumstances, Tiana had no other choice but to let it go down the way it did.

All three girls, Izzy, Tiana, and Cee Cee, lay awake in their room at the hotel in silence and hardly able to sleep. Tiana was resting on the sofa bed pullout while Izzy and Cee Cee had each taken a bed. When the digital clock on the hotel nightstand read 4:00 a.m., Tiana sat up in the sofa bed like she'd been jolted with a shock of electricity.

"Cee Cee, you asleep?" Tiana asked, shaking Celeste's arm slightly.

"Tuh, no." Celeste sucked her teeth and sighed. "Sleep? What's that?"

"Izzy, you up too?"

"Yup. I can't stop thinking about everything that's happened. It's surreal."

"Yeah, I know," Tiana agreed. "Listen, Izzy, you can come with me if you want. You don't have to go back to that asshole boyfriend of yours."

"Don't call him an asshole, Tiana," Izzy pleaded with Tiana. "You've never even met him. He's a really nice guy when you get to know him. He just has a nasty temper sometimes." She wasn't sure if she was saying it more to convince Tiana or to convince herself. Izzy wasn't sure what was going to happen when she went back home to her boyfriend, Shawn; but she had missed him the entire time she had been in there, and she had high hopes that he'd been missing her too.

"Well, in case things don't turn out the way you're expecting them to, I'm writing my friend Drake's address on a piece of paper for you. I'll most likely be staying with him until I get my plan set in stone. Even if you go to him and I'm not there, he'll make sure to help you get in contact with me." Tiana reached over to the bed and handed Izzy a small piece of paper.

"Thanks, love. You're the best." Izzy truly appreciated Tiana. Since they'd met, Tiana had been kind of mentoring her and trying to get her to be stronger for herself and not rely on Shawn so much.

Shawn had been Izzy's boyfriend of three years. Two, if you didn't count the year she'd spent in the facility. He wasn't exactly the best boyfriend to her. He'd beaten her a few times and passed her around to his friends to make some quick cash when he needed. Elizabeth always did what he asked her to do because she thought that was the only way she'd prove her love and loyalty to him.

Growing up, she bounced around from foster home to foster home, never experiencing any type of real love. When she aged out of foster care at eighteen, she decided to follow in some of her fellow foster friends' footsteps and start dancing at the local strip club in downtown Flint called Déjà Vu. A year later, she met Shawn, and she had been with him since.

"A'ight, well, I guess if we aren't going to rest anyway, it's time to split up," Tiana said, getting up from the bed.

Cee Cee sat up and stretched the kinks out of her still-aching limbs. Tiana wanted to make nice with Celeste before they split up, so she walked over to Celeste's bed and sat down next to her.

"It's all going to work out, Cee Cee. Nobody knows it was us. Just like we planned. Nobody won't even suspect us. With Dr. Syed gone now and no one to block us, we going to go back and get our revenge on motherfuckers who wronged us. Just like we've been planning and talking about. It took us months to figure out how we were going to get out of that hellhole, put all of this in place, but look at us. We did it. We fucking did it, Cee," Tiana said with feeling, trying her best to rally Cee Cee.

"Yeah, you're right. I got everything in all messed up in my head. Now that we're on the outside it's all worth it," Cee Cee said, cracking a halfhearted smile.

Tiana felt better now that she had patched things up with Cee Cee. They were back on the same plan. She didn't want to part ways with Cee Cee being upset with her. She couldn't leave things on a bad note like that. Tiana smiled back, softening at the edges.

"Just remember: you mess with me, you mess with three. We don't let anyone hurt us again," Izzy stated.

"That's right," Cee Cee agreed.

"That shit kind of corny. We sound like an afterschool special," Tiana joked.

"Yeah, it does sound corny as hell." Izzy laughed. "You and Tiana stayed talking about all that shit when y'all was gone off that Klonopin and Adderall."

"You mess with me, you mess with three," Cee Cee said in a mocking voice.

"Yeah, we was high as fuck off all that shit they was giving us when we made that up," Tiana joked back. Tiana, Izzy, and Celeste laughed and hugged each other tight.

Tiana was the first to step out of the hotel room. She surveyed the surroundings and then signaled for Izzy and Celeste to come out.

Tiana gave the girls a quick pep talk. "Stick with the plan and this shit with Dr. Syed will all blow over soon." They hugged again before they parted ways. The girls had their mission on their minds, and nothing else mattered.

Chapter 5

There was one more person Tiana needed to see right away before she made her way back to her old neighborhood. She hadn't even told Celeste and Izzy about her plan on this one, but once it was said and done, she would let them know that there was one less person they had to worry about.

Tiana knew that her father would've warned her against going to deal with a hit alone since she hadn't carefully prepared like she had been taught. Tiana didn't care. She felt a gnawing urgency for revenge against this person almost as much as she had felt for Dr. Syed.

Tiana couldn't focus on anything else until she paid a visit to Daniel Black, a perverted orderly and one of Dr. Syed's minions from Rollins Hospital. Daniel had done some unspeakable things to Tiana during her stay in the hospital, but nothing stuck out to her more than the day he had pissed on her. Tiana could still remember the feeling of the hot, acidic urine splashing onto her face and soaking her hair. After that day, she had prayed daily that she would have the opportunity to find out where Daniel lived so that one day she could see him outside of the walls of the hospital.

Tiana had been overjoyed the day her prayers were answered. It was during one of those fateful days that Daniel and Dr. Syed had performed a variety of sordid sex acts on Tiana, when she found Daniel's wallet under the bed. Tiana had lain balled up in a fetal position with her insides throbbing and her head pounding when she'd noticed the little black wallet. It had fallen from Daniel's pants pocket when he'd dropped his pants so he could force himself into Tiana's mouth and vagina, right after Dr. Syed had previously spent an hour doing the same thing. Finding the wallet had given Tiana a newfound strength and a new sense of hope. Tiana had raided the wallet before she made sure she put it back in the same place. She had gotten hold of Daniel's driver's license with his address on it and noted it before Daniel realized his wallet was gone and came looking for it. Tiana had taken the discovery of the wallet and getting Daniel's address as a sign from God, an invitation to pay Daniel a visit and pay him back.

Now, she stood in front of the address listed on the license feeling a mixture of emotions. Tiana knew Daniel worked the night shift at the hospital so she wasn't worried that she wouldn't find him at home that time of day. She touched the steak knife (courtesy of the hotel's room service) she had stuffed in the front pocket of her hoodie, and she repeated to herself the areas of the body her father told her would cause a person to bleed out the fastest. In her assessment, all she had to do was be smart, fast, and careful.

Tiana paced outside of Daniel's building until she saw someone coming out. When she saw the man exiting, Tiana slid her hood over her head and put her head down so the man couldn't see her face.

"Oh, goodness, finally. I forgot my keys at work, and I have to pee so badly. Thank you for holding the door," Tiana said sweetly, using the most proper English she could manage. She was sure to keep her head down and avoid eye contact with the man as she slipped through the door. He mumbled something to her like he was annoyed, but he didn't stop her from going into the building.

Smart man, because you woulda got it today.

"Apartment three-D," Tiana huffed as she opted to take the stairs up instead of the elevator. Once she made it to the right floor, Tiana stopped for a few seconds and took three deep, cleansing breaths.

"You can do this by yourself, Tiana. You have to do this," she spoke to herself.

Tiana raised the knocker on Daniel's door and slammed it down three times, silently praying that he was home. She felt sweat running a race down her back. She shifted her weight from one foot to the other. Suddenly her bladder felt like it was going to burst, and her nerves were on edge.

After a few moments, she listened to the locks clicking on the other side of the door. The hairs on her neck and arms stood up. *Yes!*

She swallowed hard and silently rattled off in her head what she had practiced to say. Then she thought, *This dumb nigga ain't even ask who was at the door.* Finally, she heard the final lock click. The door to the apartment swung open, and Tiana looked up into the face of her next mark.

"What the fuck are you doing here?" Daniel growled, shock registering on his face and nervousness dancing in his voice.

Tiana blinked wildly for a few seconds before her brain sent the right message to her tongue. "I came to see you because I need help," Tiana said, feigning urgency by moving restlessly on her legs. "I will do whatever you ask me to do if you just help me," she pleaded, using her best acting skills.

"Wait, when the fuck you get out?" Daniel asked, tilting his head to the side and folding his face into a confused frown. "I was out on vacation for one week, and nobody said anything about you getting released before I left. I didn't see you on the monthly release list."

"Um, no. I was released by Dr. Syed. He said I was at the end of my treatment plan," Tiana lied. "Please don't turn me away. I'm all alone out here. I have no place else to go. I have no family, and I am desperate. I'll do anything. I just need a few dollars, a hot shower, and some food." Tiana continued with her lies, throwing on her best "damsel in distress" face to take her act to an all-time high. Tiana could see Daniel's eyes light up with perverted thoughts when she said she would do anything.

"Please. I just need a few hours. I am exhausted," Tiana begged.

"All right, but I gotta leave for work in a few," Daniel relented, standing aside so Tiana could come inside. A mixture of excitement and fear flitted through Tiana's stomach, causing a wave of cramps to stab through her abdomen.

"Can I use your bathroom to freshen up?" Tiana asked.

"Do what you gotta do," Daniel answered, watching her lustfully. "But remember what you promised, Miss Caldoron. I don't have to help you, so you better keep your word or else out on the streets you go. I know how stubborn you can be."

Tiana shook her head up and down acting like she understood just what he was saying. She smiled to herself as she walked through his apartment toward the bathroom. She noticed that his laptop was open on the table in his living room. Tiana made a mental note to avoid going near it or passing it just in case it had some sort of camera running on it.

"I want to thank you for letting me in. I know it seems wild that one of your crazy patients showed up at your door but, trust me, I am grateful," Tiana called out to Daniel, making her way into his bathroom.

He was saying something in response, but she couldn't hear him because she had turned on the shower. She locked the door and pulled out the steak knife she had secreted into her pants. She put it under her foot, stepped down on the blade, and broke the handle off of it.

"Too big with the handle on it. Just be careful not to cut yourself, Tiana," she whispered to herself. She looked around the bathroom for anything else she could use as a weapon, just in case things didn't go so well with the knife. Daniel was a pretty big guy so Tiana couldn't be too careful. "Shit," she cursed. There was nothing she would be able to use right away, but she had some ideas for a few things she'd spotted.

Tiana got out of her clothes and hung them on the back of the bathroom door. She would need them to stay completely clean because she didn't have anything else to wear. She stepped into the shower, quickly wetting and soaping up her body so that Daniel would be convinced that she'd actually showered. She stepped out of the water after a few seconds, grabbed a towel that was folded on a rack above the toilet, and wrapped it around her body. She took the knife blade and hid it in the roll of the towel. Tiana took in a lungful of air, blew it out, and exited the bathroom.

"That felt so good. I'm so glad you agreed to help me," Tiana sang as she came out of the bathroom wrapped in the towel. When she didn't see Daniel, she spun around, making sure he hadn't left or that he wasn't somewhere trying to sneak up on her. "Hello?" Tiana called out tentatively, taking a few steps backward.

"I'm in here!" Daniel yelled from another room. "The bedroom!"

Tiana let out a sigh of relief, then followed the sound of his voice to a back room. Her eyebrows dipped on her face when she saw him lying stark naked on his bed looking like a sloppy, fat beached seal with his dick lying like a limp noodle on his thigh.

"I helped you; now come help me with this," Daniel said, lifting his puny dick and running his hand over it, staring at Tiana with a lecherous gaze.

Tiana felt her nervousness and fear hardening into a fiery nugget of fury, but she put a fake smile on her lips anyway. She sauntered sexily over to the bed, teasing Daniel by moving the towel aside and showing him a quick glimpse of her neatly shaven mound. She had actually shaved while she was at the hotel.

"Sss, you cleaned it up real nice for daddy. I always thought you were the best looking girl in there," Daniel panted, still stroking himself. "You were the sexiest and had the best body."

Tiana bit her lip to keep herself from going off on him. She would've had no wins if she'd gotten into a fight with Daniel, who was six foot three inches and 300 pounds.

"For real? Me? Nah, I never would've guessed that," Tiana said in a throaty, seductive voice. "I would've thought you preferred Celeste or Elizabeth." She climbed onto the bed and slowly crawled toward him. The closer she got, the more she could smell that Old Spice deodorant he would always wear. The scent was giving her flashbacks of when he would pin her down and hold her arms over her head. He would then get on top of her and begin to suck and kiss on her neck. When he was done and he'd bring her back to her room, that deodorant smell would be all over her. It was taking everything inside of her to keep the act going. Tiana knew if she had had a gun at that moment, Daniel's head would've been blown off already.

"Yeah. You have that pretty, innocent girl face but you got that ruggedness about you that makes your pussy that much better," Daniel huffed, smiling and lowering his eyes hungrily.

"Good, then that will make this time all the more special," Tiana replied, her jaw stiffening and her eyes flattening into dashes. She straddled him, wearing a wicked smile on her face and evil dancing in her eyes. Daniel began breathing harder and stroking himself rougher.

"Yeah, bring it here," he panted excitedly.

"This is no fun unless you close your eyes. Let me give it to you, since all of the other times you just took it," Tiana said.

Daniel chuckled excitedly, snapping his eyes closed.

Suddenly a quick memory of Daniel forcing his wide body between her legs and his slimy dick into her desert-dry vaginal opening flashed through Tiana's mind. Tiana remembered how she had squealed from the burning pain as he drilled into her dry opening and how Daniel forced his chunky, sweaty palm over her mouth and nose, cutting off her air supply until she gave up fighting and let him have his way with her. By the time he was finished Tiana's labia was so swollen she could barely walk for days.

"Whatever floats your boat. Open eyes, closed eyes; this is your show," Daniel wheezed hungrily, anticipation of what he thought was coming taking his breath away.

Tiana looked down in disgust at his shit brown skin and the layers of fat that made up his stomach, and she felt her insides grind with nausea. Wasting no more time, she swiftly flicked the towel from her body and retrieved the knife blade. She was so incensed that she gripped the blade tightly, and she unwittingly cut herself. The adrenaline coursing through her body didn't allow her to feel the pain.

"Keep those eyes closed now," Tiana whispered in a low growl as she ground on top of Daniel. When he felt her bare skin touch his, he began panting and drooling like a dog.

"Yeah, that's what I'm talking about," he gasped, getting ready to open his eyes.

"Uh, uh, uh. Keep those eyes closed," Tiana warned, as her legs tightened around him. She felt his erect dick pressing on her clit and the skin-to-skin contact fueled the maniacal thoughts running through her mind. She wished she had a bigger knife or maybe a chainsaw. Daniel tried to move so that he could enter her.

"Ut un, un. Let me do all the work," Tiana scolded. "Now, do you remember the first time you fucked me?" she asked, her voice hoarse with anger.

Daniel shook his head up and down in the affirmative. "It . . . it wasn't my choice to do it like that. I mean, I would've preferred to, um, you know, do it like this. But, um, Dr. S made us do that, you know, act rough with y'all so that we would risk being in trouble if we ever told on him. I . . . didn't like to do it like that. You know, hitting y'all, forcing y'all, and tying y'all down. None of that was my idea," Daniel stammered. He tried to open his eyes again, but Tiana quickly warned him against it.

"Oh, no? You didn't like forcing yourself on us, huh?" Tiana repeated. "What about running up in Celeste while she was still bleeding from that botched abortion y'all did on her? Or, what about hogtying Izzy and fucking her in the ass until she bled and couldn't shit for a week? You didn't like none of that?"

Daniel shifted uncomfortably, but Tiana pressed her weight down on him. "Well, I hope you enjoyed it, and I hope there are little girls for you to rape in hell," she growled, raising the knife blade and driving it into Daniel's jugular vein with the accuracy of a surgeon.

"Oh, shit!" Daniel squawked. His eyes shot open in shock. He threw his hands up and attempted to grab for Tiana's neck. She snaked her head away from his grasp and quickly twisted the knife blade to make sure she not only hit the external jugular but the internal one, too.

"Ahh!" Daniel gagged, his hands instinctively grabbing at his own neck. Tiana stood at the side of the bed and watched as his body bucked wildly. Daniel rolled around, trying to remove the knife blade from his neck, but Tiana could see that he was getting weak. Blood gushed from his neck and soaked the entire bed.

Tiana remembered her father telling her that it takes about two minutes for a person to bleed to death if the internal jugular vein is cut, which is larger than the external jugular vein. It was more effective if the victim was lying down like Daniel was. Tiana was hoping she had hit Daniel's carotid artery, too, because she knew he would bleed to death in one minute if she did.

"You might as well stop fighting. It'll only be a few more seconds. I hope it was all worth it. You and Dr. Syed ruined me. Y'all turned me into a fucking monster who can't go back to being an innocent little girl. Y'all turned me into an abused one," Tiana told him, her voice eerily calm. She cocked her head to the side and watched blood bubble up out of Daniel's mouth like a geyser. He let out a few more ghastly choking noises before he finally asphyxiated on his own blood. Tiana gagged a few times as the smell of the piss and shit that leaked from Daniel's body got to her. She knew the complete release of bodily fluids meant Daniel was dying. A smile curled on her lips as she took a sick sense of enjoyment watching the life leave his body.

When Daniel went completely still, Tiana went to work making sure she didn't leave any traces of herself behind. "Shit," she cursed, remembering that she had cut her finger on the knife blade. Tiana couldn't be sure that she hadn't mixed her blood with his, but she also knew she couldn't focus on that now.

She raced into the bathroom and retrieved Daniel's toilet plunger and, as a final "fuck you," Tiana went over to his naked body, took the plunger stick, and forced it into Daniel's anus.

"You like to fuck little girls, bitch? Now this little girl fucked you back," Tiana said through gritted teeth as she pushed the stick deeper and deeper, until Daniel's insides kept her from pushing it any farther. Tiana stepped back, looked at the defiled dead man in front of her, and smiled like a lunatic proud of her handiwork.

"You were right, Daddy. This is easy when it's for the right reasons. These motherfuckers ain't ready for the hurricane that's about to come into town."

Chapter 6

Celeste pulled her hood down over her forehead and looked across the street at the familiar two-story walk-up and took a deep breath. As she took a step to cross the street, two cars whizzed by her, honking their horns. The sound of honking horns made Celeste feel a warm comfort in the center of her chest. She compared the feeling to what it would feel like when a kid came home from school to the smell of baking cookies and a sweet kiss from her smiling mother.

"Flint, oh, how I've missed you," Celeste mumbled, inhaling another lungful of the smoggy air before she darted across the street.

It was hard for Celeste to imagine herself being back on her old stomping grounds after being locked up for almost two entire years. She thought she'd never get out of the hospital and away from Dr. Syed. It felt damned good to be free. Now she knew how all of the dudes her father loaned money to felt when they got released from prison.

Celeste's father was a very successful loan shark. He had clients throughout the city and had been in business for over twenty years. He was a second-generation Italian American and was groomed to take over the "family business" from a very young age. His father, Celeste's grandfather, started out loaning money to low-income immigrants who were struggling to find jobs. They would get loans and pay them back at 10 percent interest. When his father died and he took over the business, he decided to expand the money lending to practically anyone, and he increased the interest rate to 50 percent. With the unemployment rate in Flint going up after some of the car manufacturing warehouses went overseas, it was very easy for him to get clients.

But he quickly learned that not everyone had intentions of paying him back, so he hired a handful of big guys to make sure clients made their required payments. His name and reputation spread throughout Flint like wildfire and people knew better than to mess with Louis Sorrentino. He was ruthless when it came to getting his money back, and he played only by his rules. His business kept flourishing as the years went on and his pockets just kept getting fatter. He knew better than to keep all of his eggs in one basket, so he eventually started an escorting business.

He hired girls of all different races to go out with lonely men and women in need of a pretty face to accompany them to birthday parties, job promotions, or just one-on-one dinners. For whatever reason, this business seemed to attract mostly cops, judges, and attorneys, which was great for his other business because now he had connections that would help keep him out of trouble if clients ever tried to rat on him.

Just when he thought things could not get any better, he met Marie, Celeste's mother. Marie came to him broke, desperate, and inexperienced. She was young and looking for a way to make money. Someone gave her his information and told her he was always looking to hire girls, and she decided to meet with him and ask for a job. Marie was an exotic beauty. She had mesmerizing eyes and a dazzling smile that lit up a room. As soon as Louis saw her, he knew he'd make her his wife. They married within a year of meeting and Celeste was born four years later.

When Celeste was born, Louis fell completely in love with his daughter. She was the apple of his eye, and he would do anything for her. As far as he was concerned, she could do no wrong, and she was his little angel.

Cee Cee learned from a very young age that she could get away with pretty much anything by playing the sweet and innocent role. Growing up in a lavish two-story house nestled in Woodcroft Estates, she would run rampant all over the house while her nanny chased after her, begging her to stop. She would break expensive vases or statues, paint on the walls, and create the biggest messes for the nanny to clean up. When the nanny complained to her father, all Cee Cee would have to do was pout and say it was an accident, and all was forgiven. The nanny was never allowed to punish or reprimand her, so Cee Cee pretty much did whatever she wanted. She went through nannies almost every month because they couldn't handle her energy and crazy antics.

Her mother would hear all the ruckus but never cared enough to intervene. She never had time to spare for little Cee Cee. She always seemed to be running out of the house for a hair or nail appointment, a workout session with her personal trainer, or a spa day. On days she wasn't pampering herself, she would be preparing to go out to lunch, then shopping with friends, or to a charity or fundraiser of some sort. Cee Cee would sometimes ask to go with her, but Marie almost always said no. The only time she would agree to bring her daughter with her somewhere was if it was to her benefit. For example, if it was a mother-daughter brunch or a public event where she knew the press would be snapping pictures, she'd make sure to bring Cee Cee so people would see her wholesome motherly side. Cee Cee wasn't a dumb kid. She knew her mother was just using her for attention. Either way, she didn't care. She loved to play her princess role, and she played it well.

Cee Cee did a little shake in an attempt to get rid of the jitters that had her feeling like she was standing on the edge of a skyscraper about to fall off. She didn't know why she was so nervous standing outside of her house. Then it dawned on her that this would be the first time she'd be in the house since her father had been killed.

When the door opened, she craned her neck to look up at a tall, monstrous man with a barrel chest and a huge square chin.

"What?" the man growled, his eyes covered in black shades even though he was indoors.

"I'm looking for my mother, Marie," Cee Cee sassed as the giant scowled at her. She knew he was the paid security, but he didn't scare her. Celeste smirked at the idea of having paid security at their house. Her father never paid security guards. He refused to look like a weakling who needed to hire protection. Louis Sorrentino's reputation preceded him, and he stood on his own. Sometimes Cee Cee wished he would've had a security team; maybe he would still be alive.

The man attempted to close the door in Cee Cee's face, but she quickly stuck her foot between the door and the wall. "You don't have to close it," she grumbled. "Once you tell her it's her daughter I'm sure I'll be cleared to enter the castle," she said snidely.

Cee Cee could hear the security mumbling something to someone inside. After a few minutes, the door opened fully. "Oh, shit. Look who came home. The prodigal daughter has returned from the dark side," Vinny, her father's old business partner, sang sarcastically. "Come on in."

The security didn't bother to pat her down. Cee Cee guessed they were sleeping on her, which was just what she wanted them to do. She'd also learned from a young age to never let people see your true intentions because you never knew who you could trust. Her father had sent her to shooting lessons as soon as she was old enough to sign her up for it.

"Where's my mother?" Cee Cee asked flatly, walking farther inside, ignoring Vinny's smart remarks about her. It didn't take long for her to get the answer to her questions. Marie was making her way down the spiral staircase just as Cee Cee got to the marble top table that stood in the entryway beneath a crystal chandelier.

"Wow," Marie blurted when she reached Celeste, surprise registering on her face like newly applied makeup.

"Hello to you too," Cee Cee muttered, rolling her eyes. Her mother still looked as good as she had when she was twenty years old. Marie had beautiful, clear, wrinkle-free, smooth skin. Her hair fell in long jet-black ringlets around her face and down her back. Marie's curvaceous, hourglass physique hadn't changed over the years and even after birthing her daughter she still had flat abs. Marie had taken to wearing all black ever since Sorrentino's death, so she gave off the vibe of a biker maiden and not a mother type.

Cee Cee did notice one change: her mother no longer wore the tattoo on her wrist of her and Louis's names intertwined in the infinity symbol. It had been replaced with a large blossoming blue lotus flower instead.

Fucking traitor! Cee Cee screamed in her head. *My father hasn't been dead a full two years, and you've already gotten rid of your matching tattoos.*

"I didn't mean it like that, Celeste. It's just no one from that place called me to say you were better . . . you know . . . your depression," Marie recovered, walking over and giving Cee Cee a dry, perfunctory hug. Cee Cee's body stiffened uncomfortably under her mother's touch. She shrugged away from Marie, causing her mother to shrink away from her. They had never been good at exchanging affection or pleasantries, even when Cee Cee was a little girl.

"When did you get released?" Marie asked as she readjusted her blouse.

"What does it matter, Mom? It's not like you cared anyway. Don't play the role of a concerned mother now," Cee Cee snapped.

"That's not true, Celeste. Of course I care." Marie put her hand over her chest and looked at her daughter with hurt in her eyes.

"Oh, please, Ma. Save your dramatics for one of your charity events. You didn't care about how I was doing in there." Celeste rolled her eyes.

"I obviously—"

"Obvious? You want to talk about obvious?" Celeste spat, causing her mother to snap her mouth shut. "The only thing you made obvious was how much you didn't care when you didn't once visit me after you locked me away. You don't give a fuck about what I do," Celeste hissed, her eyes flattening into dashes.

"Well, I didn't visit you because there's been a lot of things going on here that have been keeping me busy," Marie stated very matter-of-factly.

"Oh, yeah, like what? Betraying your dead husband by making his partner your new little boyfriend? And to add insult to injury, you move him into the house and get Dad's tattoo covered up?"

"Boyfriend?" Vinny interrupted. "I ain't nobody's boyfriend," he said with a wide, sly smirk spreading on his face.

Celeste froze for a moment, and her heart dropped at the realization of what he had just said. She looked from Vinny to Marie, but Marie was looking to the ground to avoid making eye contact with Celeste.

"Mom. Please tell me it's not what I think it is," she said, shaking her head left to right.

Marie didn't say a word. Instead, she left Celeste standing there looking confused as she simply walked out of the room.

Vinny took a step and leaned in toward Celeste's face. "You might as well start calling me Daddy," he whispered in her ear.

Chapter 7

Tiana slowly walked up the front porch, stepped up on top of the concrete banister to the right of the door, leaned her body over a spiked piece of wrought iron, and tapped out a code on the large window.

Tap. Tap. Pause. Tap. Tap. Tap. Pause. Tap.

"Who?" a voice boomed from behind the window after a few moments.

Tiana smiled when she recognized the voice, but she didn't answer fast enough.

"Who the fuck is it?" the familiar voice shot.

"Open the fucking door, Drake!" she called out, leaning her face closer to the window. Although Tiana hadn't said her name she knew her childhood best friend, Drake, recognized her knock code and her voice. Tiana couldn't see him, and he couldn't see her, but they both knew that the other was smiling.

Tiana shoved her shaking hands deep into her pants pockets and shifted her weight from one foot to the other as she waited for Drake to open the door. Her stomach fluttered when she heard the locks clicking. She wasn't nervous about seeing Drake; she was nervous about why she'd come to see him and the obstacles that were ahead of her.

"Gotdamn, my dreams have come true," Drake crooned as he pulled back the door with a beaming and bright smile on his face.

Tiana blushed as she looked into his handsome car-amel-colored face. Drake was still one handsome dude. Tiana rushed into him with outstretched arms and a smile so wide Drake could see all thirty-two of her teeth. Drake bear-hugged her, lifted her off of her feet, and spun her around. "Mmmm, damn, baby girl, I missed the fuck out of you," Drake murmured into the skin of Tiana's neck. His warm breath sent a few heated sparks down Tiana's spine. Having a best friend who looked like a men's magazine model was not easy.

Tiana was on the brink of tears, she was so happy to see him too. She knew if she cried Drake wouldn't let her live it down. They'd been teasing one another about who was the weakest since they were five years old. Where they came from crying was the biggest sign of weakness.

Drake placed Tiana back on her feet, laced his fingers through hers, and pulled her farther inside. He shut the doors and employed the ten locks he had on them. Then he pulled Tiana down the long, dimly lit hallway to his apartment door.

"What the fuck is up, Tee?" Drake chimed, referring to Tiana by the nickname he'd made for her when they were kids.

"I'm fucking back out in the world, that's what's up. I'm here because you're the only person who cared enough to write to me and send me shit after that bitch doctor sent me away to that piece of shit hospital. She signed that paperwork, put me out with the trash, and never looked back," Tiana said as they stopped together right in front of Drake's door at the first-floor apartment.

He owned the entire building but had tenants on the other floors. Drake had done well for himself, seeing that he was the son of a deceased heroin addict and a prison lifer. Drake had started hustling when he was ten and had risen through the street ranks. He had made a name for himself in the streets and was making more money than a little boy from the hood like him could've ever imagined.

Before opening the front door, Drake turned around to take in an eyeful of his friend, whom he'd always loved from the day he laid eyes on her. He looked at Tiana lovingly, but then he scrunched up his face when she moved into the light that hung above the door.

Drake balked. "Damn, Tee, you look like you been through hell or just came back from it. What's with the all black? And the dirty hoodie? And why fuck you lose so much weight? Your clothes is hanging off of you. When's the last time you combed your hair? How'd you get the cuts on your face and hands? What the fuck were you doing in that hospital? Fighting the devil n'shit? You look rough as fuck."

Tiana pulled the sleeves on her sweater to try to cover her hands. With the commotion of her and the girls finally getting released and the excitement of coming back to Flint, her appearance had been the last thing on her mind. With him pointing it all out, she was feeling a bit embarrassed.

She wasn't about to let him see it, though. She twisted her lips with a smirk of satisfaction. "Well, damn, I didn't know you were gonna be looking at me so hard. I been in a psych ward for more than a year. You think that shit is like a resort? You think they had a hair salon and little clothing and shoes boutiques for me to buy outfits so I could look all cute and pretty at the group meetings?" She looked down at her worn-out sneakers and chuckled a little. "You're right, though. I have been fighting the devil. But I beat his ass, and now I'm back!" She and Drake both smiled and leaned in to give each other daps.

"A'ight, well, I'm still not feeling all this shit. We need to go shopping right fucking now. And this hair, nah. I'm used to my girl having her hair smelling and looking like it belongs on a hair magazine cover. Remember how your dad used to always call you his cover girl?"

Tiana's face went dark when Drake mentioned her father. Drake immediately regretted bringing him up. "I'm sorry, Tee. I didn't mean to get you upset and thinking about your dad."

"No, it's okay, Drake. I think about him all the time anyway," she admitted. "I do remember him calling me that and how much I hated it."

Drake smiled at her last comment. "Yeah, you did. And you got mad at him every time he said it, too. You were too much of a tomboy to be called a cover girl," he mocked her.

"Shut up!" she replied as she gave him a playful shove. "Well, are you gonna let me in or are we gonna stand here by the door all day?"

"No, I ain't letting you in just yet. Right now I'm gonna go get my keys, and me and you are heading out for the day. I'm gonna take you to Nina's to get your hair done. You need a trim and possibly even some highlights up in that mess on top of your head right now. Then we have to get those nails of yours fixed up. I was planning on going to pick up some sneakers for myself at the mall later so might as well have you pick out some outfits and kicks too."

Tiana was surprised to hear Drake go on about doing all these things men usually avoided. She never remembered him being the type to care or even know about women's hair, nails, and clothing. "Um, Drake, since when do you know about all this girl stuff?" she questioned him.

"Since I know how I like my women to look." He smirked and winked at her before running inside to grab his keys.

Tee felt herself blushing. She remembered when Drake's voice started changing and he got tall and athletic out of nowhere. She didn't have many friends in school, especially female friends. But in tenth grade, girls started trying to talk to her and act like they were interested in getting to know her. She quickly realized that all these girls were just pretending to want to be friends with her because they wanted to ask her questions about Drake. She found it hilarious how these girls had such big crushes on him because to her he was like a brother. She just didn't see him in that light. It wasn't until their senior year that she began seeing him differently.

It was Friday night, and they had made plans to go catch a movie. Tiana got to his house early, and his mother told her he was in the bathroom taking a shower. Tiana excused herself and went to Drake's room to wait for him.

Drake's mom was on the couch high off of something. She was used to seeing her son coming home with girls all the time. Usually, she was too high or drunk to care, but she had noticed that Drake treated Tiana different from the rest. She knew Tiana was special to him because she was the only one he'd ever let in his bedroom. All the other girls never made it past the living room where he'd usually have them fuck him or suck him. His mother never complained or said anything to him because, at this point, he was the one paying all the bills, and he even gave her some money from time to time, and she wasn't about to mess that up for herself.

Tiana was sitting on his bed when Drake walked in wearing nothing but a towel. Tiana had no idea he looked this good under the clothes he wore. His skin was a perfect chocolate brown complexion and looked silky smooth. He had a broad, defined back, muscular arms, and a perfect six pack. Tiana was mesmerized by the little droplets of water sliding down his chest, and she was surprised to see perfect little curls all over it. Up until that moment, Tiana had never realized she found chest hair on a man attractive. Up until that moment, Tiana hadn't realized she found men attractive, period! Not to say that she was into girls, but Tiana had never really taken notice of guys like that.

"Tee! I didn't think you'd be here so early," Drake said nonchalantly as he walked over to his dresser to grab some boxers. He didn't seem fazed at all that he was standing in front of her with practically no clothes on.

"Yeah, my bad. I had nothing else to do so I figured I'd come over and we could hang out until it was time to leave. I'll wait for you in the living room while you get yourself ready, though," Tiana said as she started heading toward the door.

"You don't have to leave. It's cool. I just need to get dressed, and we can go. Maybe we could get some ice cream on the way over." He slid his boxers on and let the towel fall to the floor.

Tiana took a seat back on the bed and felt very awkward watching him. She looked on as he put the rest of his clothes on. Once dressed, he lotioned up and sprayed himself with Fahrenheit cologne. Tiana never noticed how well that cologne mixed with his natural scent. She closed her eyes and took a deep breath. As she took it all in, all of a sudden, she felt a tingling between her legs and she didn't understand what it was that she was feeling.

She ran out of the room in a panic without giving a word of explanation that night. She went home and didn't call or talk to Drake until a few days later.

"Okay, I'm ready to go," Drake interrupted her thoughts.

"All right, let's get going then." Tiana looked up at him and smiled.

"Let's get you all dolled up, cover girl."

Chapter 8

Elizabeth had been standing at the stop sign staring at the building across the street for almost thirty minutes. As much as she just wanted to walk right up to the front door and knock, for some reason she felt scared and anxious to be so close to a moment she had been thinking about for so long now. Being that he hadn't gone to the hospital to check on her since the night she was admitted into the hospital a year and a half ago, she wasn't sure how he'd react when he opened the door and saw her standing there. Things hadn't exactly ended on a good note the last time they had seen each other.

"Her vitals are dropping, and her pulse is slowing down!" the nurse yelled out. *"If we don't get her stabilized we might lose her."*

Izzy could barely make out what was being said. She felt like she was having an out-of-body experience. She wasn't sure if she was dreaming or if everything was happening in real time. The last thing she could really remember was Shawn screaming at her because his chicken was cold.

He was going on about how useless she was and how she couldn't do anything right. She didn't think his chicken was cold. She had just taken it out of the oven five minutes before serving it to him. She wasn't listening to much of what he was saying because her cramps were so bad they almost felt like contractions. The Percocet she had taken earlier didn't seem to be helping much, and all she wanted to do was lie down. She didn't have the energy to say much to him so she figured the next best thing was to just nod along to everything he was saying so he could calm down and they could get on with the night.

"You fucking stupid bitch! Are you even listening to a word I'm saying?" Shawn spat at her.

"Yes, yes, I'm listening, baby," Izzy pleaded with him.

"Then answer the fucking question." Shawn got in her face and pinned her between himself and the kitchen counter.

"Um . . ." Izzy had no idea what to say. She knew things were about to get a lot worse for her. "Baby, I promise I was listening to everything you said. I just didn't hear your last question because—"

Before Izzy could finish her sentence, Shawn's fist landed on the side of her face like a hammer. Almost immediately her left ear started ringing, and the room began to spin.

"You fucking bitch!" Shawn was landing punch after punch in between his words. "You think I'm gonna let you disrespect me in my motherfucking house?"

Izzy was no match for his fists, and her legs gave way, causing her to fall to the floor on her side. She balled herself up in the fetal position and prayed for it to be over soon.

Shawn lost himself in his kicks and punches. When he finally stopped, he realized Izzy was a bloody mess, and she was completely passed out. Her eyes were almost swollen shut. He tried to get her to wake up so she could wash herself off and get to bed. But no matter how hard he shook her, she would not open her eyes. He knew she needed medical attention, but he had no idea how he'd be able to explain how she got all the bruises on her.

Then it dawned on him to put her in the car, and drive toward Déjà Vu, the strip club Izzy worked at. He'd drive a little bit past the club and leave her on South Dort Highway so somebody could see her and call 911. If he did that, then he could skip town to his brother's house and use him as an alibi just in case she had diarrhea of the mouth.

Before following through with that plan, Shawn decided to try to get her to wake up. He dashed into the bathroom and ran a cold bath.

"Yeah, this should wake this bitch up. How the fuck she gonna pass out on me while I'm trying to teach her a lesson?" he mumbled to himself. He went back into the kitchen, grabbed a chunk of her hair, and dragged her into the tub. He kept shaking her in the bathtub and slapping her cheeks until she finally seemed to be waking up.

Izzy slowly began to come to. Woozy and aching all over, Izzy felt her body tensing up from the cold water. She couldn't help but groan from the pain she was feeling all over. Her face was stinging, and her eyes were throbbing. She couldn't see at all from her left eye, but from her right eye, she could see Shawn towering over her in the bathtub.

"Bitch, how fucking dare you disrespect me and fall asleep while I'm talking to you! Look at me when I'm talking before I fuck you up some more."

Izzy tried to speak but the blood dripping from her swollen, busted lip and the pain in her mouth stopped her from being able to utter a single word. All she could do was try to look up at him with her good eye and try to listen and do whatever he asked her to do.

"Now clean yourself up and get my dinner right."

Izzy attempted to get up by grabbing the shower curtains, but she was so disoriented that she accidentally *grabbed him by his dreads and pulled him into the tub with her. He quickly jumped out of the tub, cocked his right hand back, and swung right at Izzy's face like a bat to a baseball.*

"So you think you can fight me, bitch? It's on!" Shawn slammed a final blow to her soft, unsuspecting stomach. This both woke her up and knocked the breath out of her. When she was able to catch her breath again, Izzy felt her adrenaline pumping, and suddenly she had all the energy she needed to bolt out of the room and leave.

With her one good eye, she made her way out of the bathroom, leaving a trail of water behind her. Shawn ran after her but slipped on the wet floor.

"You disrespectful bitch! I'ma kill you when I catch you!"

She could hear Shawn screaming not far behind her. Izzy reached the front door and ran out into the snowy winter night. Scared he'd soon reach her, Izzy didn't bother to see if there were any cars coming and she hurriedly ran out into the street. Just as she stepped into the second lane, someone was speeding down the road in a four-wheel ATV.

The kid in the ATV was going too fast and wasn't able to slow down in time to avoid slamming into Izzy. He didn't hit her head-on, but he did hit her hard enough that Izzy's body bounced off of the ATV and fell back onto the front of the building she was trying to run away from. Scared that he'd be in a lot of trouble, the kid quickly sped off and disappeared down the road.

Shawn saw the whole thing and couldn't believe he'd gotten so lucky. Now he had the perfect scenario to take her to the hospital emergency room. When he got to the hospital, he told the doctors that she had been suicidal for days and that she had tried to kill herself by jumping in front of a car. He told them she'd been cutting and hurting herself for some time and he didn't know what to do with her anymore.

After a few hours of coming in and out of conscious-ness, Izzy finally woke up to see Shawn sitting in a chair beside her hospital bed. When she tried to move, she realized both of her arms and legs were attached to the bed with restraints. She tried to speak, but her mouth was dry and her throat felt very hoarse. Izzy looked over to Shawn with tears in her eyes, hoping to see a glimmer of love and affection from him but, instead, when she looked over to him she was met with a sinister smirk on his face.

He stood up and leaned into her ear, whispering, "Say anything about me, bitch, and I'll make sure those will be your last words." With that, he turned and left the room to speak to the doctors. She strained to hear what the doctors were saying to Shawn. From what she could make out, she learned that she was going to be transported to William P. Rollins facility for a psych evaluation.

That was the last time she'd seen or heard from Shawn. The entire time she was in Rollins Hospital, all she could think about was getting back to her bae. She missed being with him and wanted nothing more than to be back at home and put the last year behind them. Sure, they had their fights and arguments, but she loved him, and he was the only man who had ever taken care of her. He had let her move in with him when she had no place else to go, and he had even promised to marry her one day.

Izzy took a deep breath and ran toward the building. She knocked on the door and patiently waited for some-one to open it. She thought her heart was going to jump right out of her chest as she stood in front of the beat-up old door.

"Who is it?" Shawn yelled out as he made his way toward the door. Izzy could hear his footsteps getting closer and closer.

"Baby, it's me," was all she could muster. She didn't get a response but just then she heard locks clicking and a chain rattling. She stopped breathing for a second when the door finally opened.

Shawn stood in front of her looking handsome as ever. Even in gray sweatpants and a white T-shirt he still managed to look good. At six feet two inches tall he was built like an NFL football player. He had a naturally athletic body without having to spend hours at the gym. His caramel skin tone complemented his almond-shaped hazel eyes and really made his thick pink lips stand out. He was Jamaican, but people often assumed he was Hispanic because of his light eyes and complexion.

"Would you look what the cat dragged in," he said as he looked down at a nervous-looking Izzy.

"Hi, baby. I missed you." Izzy got on her tiptoes and extended herself to try to give Shawn a kiss, but as her face got closer to his, Shawn leaned back and pushed her off of him.

"The fuck are you doing?" he said with a scrunched-up expression.

"I just wanted to give you a kiss. I missed you, Mr. Peanuts." Mr. Peanuts was the nickname she had given him from when they first met at the strip club. He would come in about twice a week, and he always finished the entire bowl of peanuts that sat at the center of the table. He would watch her strip, and he usually paid for a private lap dance afterward. It was during those lap dances that he would whisper in her ear and make small talk with her. As much as she asked, he would never give her his name, so she eventually started calling him Mr. Peanuts.

"So you get ghost on me for a year and then come back thinking shit is gonna be cool between us just like that?" he asked her.

"Baby, I got sent up to Rollins after that night the car hit me. I tried to call you but it said your number was disconnected," she tried to explain herself to him.

"Oh, so they sent you up to the loony bin?" He chuckled.

"Yeah. They kept asking me why I jumped in front of the car. And they thought I was crazy when I told them I didn't do it on purpose."

"You better not have told them I did some shit to you."

"No, Mr. Peanuts. I would never say anything to get you in trouble like that. What happened that night was my fault anyway," she said as she looked up at him.

"You damn right it was your fault. Your ass shoulda been listening to what the fuck I was saying to you."

"Yeah, I know. I'm sorry, baby."

"Yeah, you are sorry," Shawn said to her. "But you gon' make it up to me real soon. Let's get inside. It's cold as fuck out here," Shawn said as he turned with Izzy following close behind.

Izzy looked around and realized a lot of things had changed in the apartment since she'd been gone. The house was clean and smelled like freshly baked apple pie. Sheer purple and ivory curtains hung in the living room window. Two gray pillows with purple and white flowers were neatly stacked on each corner of the black leather couch that was set right in front of the TV. She walked over to the small dining room table and saw a Paula Deen candle burning on top of a round flower-embroidered silver placemat. She saw the scent was fried apple pie and figured that's where the smell was coming from.

"Did you miss me?" Shawn crept up behind her, put his hands on her waist, and ground his hips into hers as he whispered into her ear. Izzy closed her eyes and took in the moment. She had missed him so much. His hands made their way up to her breasts, and he squeezed them while he began to kiss on the back of her neck.

"Yeah, baby, I missed you so much," she said in between breaths. Her neck was her spot, and Shawn knew that. She turned around and pulled him to her. His lips felt so good against hers. It felt so different from Dr. Syed's thin, chapped lips. She hated when Dr. Syed would go on and on kissing her because his breath always smelled and he always tasted like fresh garlic. With Shawn it was so different, though. His mouth felt warm and soft, and it tasted like fresh Listerine. Izzy moved on and started kissing him on the neck while her hands roamed all over his hard, toned chest.

She felt her pussy throbbing and her juices flowing. She couldn't remember the last time she'd gotten wet. At the hospital, Dr. Syed would ram himself inside of her while she was dry as a desert. He didn't seem to care, though, because he would slam in and out of her groaning and moaning telling her how good it felt. Meanwhile, her insides would feel like they were on fire from the dry friction of his nasty dick sliding up and down her walls.

Shawn grabbed her hands and guided them down toward his pants so she could feel his growing hard dick throbbing against them. She pulled on the string of his pants to loosen them up. His pants fell down to his ankles. To her surprise, he had no boxers on, and he just stood there with his dick pointing out like a straight arrow. By now, they had made their way toward the living room. Shawn fell back on the couch with a big smile on his face as Izzy got on her knees and grabbed his dick and gently started stroking it up and down with her hands.

"Mmm, that shit feels good," he said. Izzy looked up at him, happy to see her man smiling down at her.

"Put it in your mouth," he instructed her. Izzy wasted no time doing as she was told. She took in all ten inches of him and began to deep-throat his manhood. Once his dick was all wet and slippery, she glided one hand up and down his shaft while she sucked on the head.

"Damn, baby, you really missed this daddy dick, huh?"

Izzy kept sucking away. She kept stroking her hands up and down with her mouth following them. She licked his pre-cum when she felt a slight twitch from his pelvis area. By now her pussy was throbbing and dripping wet. She couldn't wait to get on top and start riding him, but she wanted to make sure he was fully satisfied with the head she was giving him first.

She started stroking him faster and harder with her hand while she sucked on his balls. She knew that would really get him going. She got a rhythm going as she went back and forth taking one ball in her mouth at a time while her hands slid up and down his dick. When she felt he'd had enough, she sprang up and started sucking on the head again while her hands slid back down and caressed his balls.

"Oh my God! You know how to suck some dick, baby," Shawn said as he grabbed a handful of her head and started guiding it up and down. Izzy almost gagged from how hard his dick was hitting the back of her throat, but she knew better than to kill the moment.

Instead, she pulled back and stood up so she could start taking her clothes off. She started dancing and shaking her ass in front of him as if there was song playing for her to dance to. She turned her back to him and made her cheeks jiggle as she bent over to the floor and touched her toes. She came back up and slowly pulled her pants down. She turned back around and took her shirt off. Her titties were snug in their bra, but she couldn't wait to get them out and into his mouth. She figured she'd get to that eventually because, right now, her main focus was to get him inside of her.

She climbed onto the couch and straddled him. She reached down, grabbed his dick with her left hand and slid her panties to the side with her right hand. She purposely made his dick slide against her opening so he could feel how wet she was before he entered her. When she couldn't wait anymore, she pushed his member inside of her. The feel of his hard, thick dick going into her took her breath away. She started bouncing up and down. She arched her back and gyrated her hips back and forth with each thrust.

Shawn grabbed at each side of her panties and ripped them off. Having her panties ripped off of her only turned her on more. With no underwear on, she could feel her clit rubbing against his bare skin. She began to do her Kegels so he could feel her pussy walls tightening on him. He pulled her in closer so he could reach his arms around her and take her bra off. He quickly found the clasp, unfastened it, and threw the bra across the room. Izzy didn't miss a beat and kept doing what she was doing. With her titties out, she started bouncing on him harder. She loved the way her breasts felt as they went up and down while she was fucking.

"You missed this pussy, daddy?" she asked him as she rode him.

"Yeah, I missed it," Shawn replied. He loved the way she looked when she was riding him. With her thick thighs straddled around his legs, her tiny waist, and big ass, she could pass for a porn star. She had small B-cup breasts, but they were perfectly round and firm. Her nipples looked like small little Hershey's Kisses and tasted just as good, too. Shawn had always been more of an ass man, so her having small titties didn't matter much to him. Izzy began to pick up the pace, and Shawn felt himself about to explode.

"Izzy, I'm about to cum." Izzy didn't stop and kept going faster and faster until Shawn exploded inside of her. She stopped and just stayed sitting on him with his penis still resting within her. She could feel his piece pulsing inside of her. She felt fulfilled that she had been able to satisfy her man.

After a few minutes of sitting in silence, she got off him and went to the bathroom to grab him a washrag to clean himself off with. While he did that, she decided to freshen herself up. There was a lot of catching up to do between them so she figured she'd take a shower, and run to the grocery store to pick up something to make for dinner.

It felt great to be back home and with the love of her life again. Now they could get on with their lives and soon get married like Shawn had promised. She took her shower and made her way to the bedroom. When she opened the top drawer of her dresser, her heart dropped. None of her things were in there anymore. There were women's items in the drawer, but none of it belonged to her. The deodorant brand was not the type that she used, and there were Victoria's Secret lotions and spray bottles that she had never purchased.

"Shawn!" she yelled out as she ran into the living room where a naked Shawn seemed to be waking up from a nap. "Whose stuff is in my drawer?"

Shawn had dozed off after busting his nut and didn't realize that Izzy had gone off to take a shower. "Oh, that's Laura's stuff," he replied nonchalantly.

"Laura? Who the fuck is Laura, Shawn?" Izzy asked with an attitude.

"Now you just wait one motherfucking minute. Watch who the fuck you talking to," Shawn snapped.

Izzy immediately changed her tone. Yes, she was mad and upset that another woman's things were in her drawer, but she also knew better than to get Shawn mad.

"I'm sorry, baby. I didn't mean to come at you like that. But who is Laura and why are her things in my drawer?" she asked as nicely as she possibly could.

"That's my girl."

"Your girl as in what?"

"My girl as in my girlfriend." Shawn spoke to her like she was stupid.

"Your girlfriend?" Izzy felt like someone had just poured hot water over her head. Her heart dropped, and she felt like she was about to have a panic attack.

"Yes, my fucking girlfriend. What? You thought I was just gonna sit here and wait for you to come back this whole time?" Shawn came at her with an attitude. "A nigga got needs and shit that needs to be taken care of. My food needs to be cooked, my house needs to be kept clean, and my clothes need be washed," he stated while grabbing at his finger with each demand as if he was counting.

"But, I thought you loved me. How could you move somebody else into our house like that, Shawn?" Izzy was in complete disbelief of what he had just told her.

"Our house?" Shawn started laughing a maniacal laugh. "This is my fucking house and nobody else's. Your bitch ass must still be having mental problems if you thing this was ever our house. I let you live here for a little bit, but this was never your house."

Izzy had no words after hearing what Shawn was saying to her. Her heart felt like it had been broken into a million pieces. All the beatings and rapes that she had endured at Rollins would never amount to the pain she was feeling right now after hearing that Shawn had moved on and had somebody else.

"Listen, Izzy, it was good while it lasted but it's over," he said to a Izzy as she stood there wrapped in a towel.

Izzy was so far gone in her mind. She just stood there staring at the wall in front of her.

"Yo! Earth to Izzy!" Shawn snapped his fingers in front of her to try to get her to snap back to reality.

Izzy's eyes filled with tears and she finally reacted and looked over at him. "I don't understand. We just made love and you told me you missed me," she reasoned with him.

"Nah, baby girl. I told you I missed that pussy. And I did, which is why I wanted to feel it one more time. Now that I did, it's time for you and that pussy of yours to get the fuck outta my house."

"But I have no place else to go, Shawn. You know you're all I have," she cried to him.

"Well, you shoulda thought about that before you decided to get yourself hurt and sent up to Rollins for a year." Shawn looked over at a crying Izzy and felt a pang of sympathy for her. "A'ight, I'll tell you what. Laura doesn't get home until close to five in the evening. You can put on one of her outfits so you could get fresh and I'ma let you stay here until four o'clock today. That oughta give you enough time to figure out what your next move is. But, after that, you gots to go." With that, Shawn walked out of the room and left Izzy standing there looking confused and heartbroken.

Chapter 9

"I like what you've done with the place. Nobody would have ever guessed from the outside that this shit was decorated like an expensive penthouse inside," Tiana complimented as she whirled around taking in the beautiful dark ebony hardwood floors, the plush Italian leather furniture, the ultra modern barstools, Art Deco artwork on the walls, and the huge flat-screen televisions that gave the place a sports lounge feel.

"A real bachelor's pad," Tiana followed up, picking up a glass-encased autographed Derek Jeter baseball that had to be worth a good bit of money.

"You know how I do, baby." Drake smiled, winking at her. "The streets have showed me mad love." He opened his arms wide. "And I show those motherfuckers love right back."

"Where can I put my bags for now?" Tiana asked, holding up the bags of clothes she was carrying from their shopping adventure at the mall.

"You can put them right in the guest room. It's down the hall to the left," he said, pointing down the hall.

"Listen, I really appreciate you taking me out and hooking me up today. Promise I'll get you back as soon as I'm up on my feet."

"Tiana, stop it. You know I ain't looking to get nothing back from you. Shit, I owe you two birthdays from the last two years that you ain't been around so consider it super-late gifts."

"Thanks, Drake. You're the best," Tiana said as she leaned in and planted a soft kiss on his cheek.

A few seconds of silence passed between them before Tiana walked down the hallway to put her things away. As she made her way back to the living area, Tiana thought it was best to stop beating around the bush and let Drake know this wasn't just a pleasure visit.

"Yo, Drake, I need your help." Tiana sighed, flopping down on the dark chocolate leather recliner. "I didn't come here to see you just to say what's up." She figured getting to the point was the best way to get what she needed as fast as possible.

"A'ight. What's really good then? Anything for you, ma."

"I hate to ask, but as soon as I am on my feet I will repay you—" Tiana started.

"C'mon with that bullshit, man. We don't even roll like that. From Now & Laters and quarter waters to visits up north and psych hospitals, we always had each other's backs. What's mine is yours, you already know," Drake cut her off.

Tiana parted a warm smile. The love she felt for Drake hung in the air like an iridescent cloud in one of those fairytale books.

"Well, I got some things I need to take care of and some people I need to see," Tiana said seriously. "Everybody thought when my father got murked shit was over. I was locked away against my will, and nobody knows I'm out yet, but they will all know soon enough. I will not be able to rest until I get my payback. You know better than anybody how much my father cared about his people. He did his dirt, but it was all business. He took care of his own."

"A'ight, I'm here to help you in any way I can," Drake said, moving to the edge of the couch to show his interest in what she was saying. "Marquez was my hero, so anything I can do to help you, I'm down."

"Well, the first thing I need to do is to locate some people," Tiana said, pulling out a crumpled piece of paper. "I know you got connects everywhere, so this shouldn't be that hard for you to figure out."

Tiana had had a lot of time to kill at Rollins and had meticulously created her list. She and Celeste had each created their list of people they wanted to get their revenge on. Izzy hadn't made one because she said she didn't have any people she needed to get back at. But Tiana and Celeste were on a mission to get their revenge on people. They sat together during their time at Rollins and went on and on about how, when they got out, they were going to get all these people back for wronging them. Tiana wasn't sure if Celeste was serious about her plans, but Tiana's was a real hit list, and she had every intention of going out and killing these people.

Drake examined the paper Tiana had handed him. It contained two lists of names: one column had stars next to the names, and others had Xs next to them. Drake squinted and read the names silently. The names with the Xs next to them he recognized. He blanched and reared back in his seat with his lips pressed tightly together.

"What? Why the look?" Tiana asked him.

"That's a heavy-ass list right there," Drake warned, gazing at Tiana seriously. "You got some pretty dangerous motherfuckers on there. Even people I don't fuck around with, Tiana," he said, shaking his head from left to right while rubbing his chin.

"Yeah, all of the same motherfuckers who set my father up and had him killed," Tiana said with her teeth gritted, her jaw rocking. "I'm not scared of them. They won't even know I'm coming. I'm not asking you to get your hands dirty. Just help me behind the scenes, Drake. I need addresses, hang-out spots, anything you can find out.

The other list should be easy. These people all grew up around here in Flint so I know your ID connects and shit like that can easily find their home addresses."

Drake blew out an exasperated breath. There was no use in arguing with Tiana because she was the most stubborn person he knew. "A'ight, Tee, where you want to start at?" Drake huffed, biting his bottom lip. "The lames or the street cats?"

"First, I need a place to lie low. I can't stay here because I don't want to bring unwanted attention to you and your shit. I know you got a few properties around BK. Anyplace will do. Shit, I don't care if it's a hole in the fucking wall as long as I can lock the door when I rest my head at night. I also need a few burner phones. The one and done types. I don't need money; I'll make my own once I get my feet wet," Tiana rambled, speaking like a real businesswoman.

"Oh. All of that I can help you with," Drake replied, flicking his lighter to light the end of his cigarette. Tiana knew Drake only smoked cigarettes when he had shit on his mind or he was nervous about something; other than that, his thing was two or three blunts of sour a day. "I got you. Whatever you need, I'm here. But, before we start getting down to business and revenge plots and shit, first, *amiga,* we need to celebrate your spoiled ass being home," Drake joked, walking back over to Tiana and placing a bottle of Luc Belaire Rare Rosé on the table in front of her. She smiled and nodded her agreement. She wasn't a big drinker but, after everything she'd been through, it was a welcomed vice.

"Hell, yeah, I could use a fucking drink," Tiana cheered, raising her hands and clapping. "If you only knew, Drake," she mumbled, leaning forward, picking up her glass and taking it to the head. "If you only fucking knew."

***

The next day, Drake stopped his smoke gray Audi A6 in front of the old, rickety wrought-iron gates that surrounded what used to be a beautiful palatial house in Grand Blanc just fifteen minutes out of downtown Flint. He turned down the music in the car, and he and Tiana stared out of the window.

"Gotdamn." Drake sucked in his breath at the sight in front of them. It was a sharp reminder of the tragic story of the Caldoron family. Tiana herself belched out a sob and clasped her hand over her mouth. It was all she could do to keep from screaming as she took in an eyeful of what used to be a place she associated with love and the good life. She stared at the disaster she used to call home, now reduced to looking like a haunted house from a bad scary movie. Dark green and brown ivy vines snaked over the dirty tan bricks choking off the beauty of the home's custom masonry. The windows were tinted with layers of dirt and the earth's elements; the tall, faded white columns that at one time had made the house look so grand now bore top-to-bottom cracks and were pockmarked with bullet holes.

"I can't believe she let all of his hard work crumble to shit. She just moved on like he never fucking existed," Tiana said through clenched teeth, swiping roughly at her angry tears. "She didn't even try to put the pieces of our lives back together. That bitch wanted to get rid of all of us."

"Your stepmother will get what's coming to her," Drake comforted her. "Your father loved you, and he was proud of you."

Tiana swallowed hard and shook her head, mad at herself that she let these tidal waves of emotions drown her. She tried to keep her memories of her father to a minimum, for fear that they would somehow fade away if she overused them, but being at the house, she couldn't help think about him.

Marquez Caldoron was so proud the day he'd brought Tiana and her stepmother to the house for the first time. "All of this for mi familia," he said after he'd given them the signal to remove their blindfolds.

Moving his family out of Flint to a 3,000-square-foot house that sat on half an acre had been a big deal for Marquez. The house was bigger than any Tiana had ever seen in her life. Her mouth dropped open at the sight.

When she first stepped out of her father's car Tiana was blown away by the tall pedestal fixtures on each side in front of the front door walkway. She had to tilt her head all the way back as she looked up at the soaring ceiling in the entryway. She couldn't believe that there was a window on the ceiling. Her dad chuckled at the sight of how excited his daughter was and then explained to her that it was called a skylight. Tiana was fifteen when they moved out there. It was surely a big difference from the small apartment Tiana had grown up in.

When the family walked throughout the house for the first time they stared wide-eyed at their new home. Marquez had already had it fully furnished with the finest imported Italian furnishings. Tiana raced up to her room, and when she stepped inside, she was amazed that her father had paid to have all of her track medals encased in a gold-trimmed shadow box.

Track was something Tiana loved to do. She had been running since she was ten and, from her very first meet, the coaches told her she was a natural-born runner. Over the years she had won many competitions and had accumulated a good amount of trophies and medals.

"I'm proud of you, mija. Always proud of you. No matter what you choose to do in life, your papi will always be proud of you," her father said from her doorway.

Now, the house looked like it hadn't been lived in for over twenty years, yet Tiana and her family lived there up until her father's murder a year and a half before. Tiana still thought about how strange it was that her stepmother hadn't been home when her father's rivals sprayed the house full of bullets, killing her father. The family was always together but, that day, her stepmother insisted on running out to a Redbox to rent a movie for all of them to watch. At twenty-two years old, Tiana rarely spent time with her dad and stepmom to do movie nights, so she wasn't planning on watching with them. And her stepmother never cared enough to spend "family time" with her and her father.

Tiana was in her room on the second level when everything happened. She heard glass breaking and what sounded like firecrackers. At first she didn't understand what was going on. She assumed the noise was coming from a TV downstairs. But when she heard voices coming from outside, she ran toward her window that overlooked the front of the house and got there just in time to see two guys falling back to the front and rear passenger's seats of a car, each with guns in their hands. The black sedan burned its tires as it peeled out and raced down the street, disappearing into the night. Tiana ran downstairs and found her dad face down on the living room floor. He had been shot multiple times and was gone by the time she got to him.

She regretted everything about that day. She often wondered how things would've turned out if she had done things differently that day. Her father had called her earlier on that day and invited her to go out to dinner with him. She turned him down because she had plans to go to the mall with Drake to pick up some sneakers. When she got home that night, she ran straight upstairs to her room without saying a word to him. She had been so excited to pick out an outfit to wear with her newest Jordans the next day that she hadn't even bothered to say hello or kiss her father good night, taking for granted she would see him the next morning.

When Tiana's stepmother returned home to the news that their house had been shot up and her husband had been killed, she screamed and wailed while the cops and paramedics were there. When everyone had gone, though, she went upstairs to shower and seemed calm and cool as a cucumber.

The next morning her stepmother was up and out of the house before Tiana had awoken. Tiana got up and felt like her world was over. She stayed in her room for days, not bothering to eat, brush her teeth, or anything. She didn't even remember her new clothes and sneakers. In fact, she never wore the sneakers she'd gotten that day. Tiana thought of them as a bad omen.

After her father's murder, Giselle, Tiana's stepmother, kept the house for close to four months but she kept telling Tiana she no longer felt comfortable in it. Giselle hadn't even removed the yellow police crime scene tape from the outside until almost a month after Marquez had been buried.

Giselle eventually opted to stay with friends back in Flint. She claimed that she was scared that her husband's killers might return to their house in Grand Blanc. Tiana had thought of that living arrangement as temporary and assumed that one day they would return home and attempt to live a normal life again. Giselle had been in her and her father's life since she was twelve and she was the closest thing to a mother she had, so she figured the best thing for her to do was to go along with whatever plans Giselle had for them. She had figured wrong.

One day her stepmother came and told her they weren't ever going back to their old house and were staying in Flint permanently. It wasn't until they'd gone back to their estate, packed, and were ready to abandon the house that Tiana discovered that they were moving in with Lobo, her stepmother's best friend who was "like a brother to her." Tiana was shocked and angered to learn that all of a sudden he was her mother's new love interest.

"It didn't even take you six full months before you started fucking other people, huh?" Tiana had said, throwing a verbal punch at Giselle that morning. Giselle had rushed into Tiana like a bulldozer and slapped her so hard she'd left finger marks on Tiana's cheek. That was the first of many explosive fights between Tiana and her stepmother.

Within six months of moving in with Lobo and Giselle, Tiana missed her father so much that one night she went into the bathroom, said three Hail Marys, and slit both of her wrists so deep she had exposed the bone in one. She had narrowly missed successfully committing suicide. Lobo had found her swimming in a pool of her own blood just in time to save her life. Giselle wasted no time committing Tiana to the psych ward at Rollins.

White, hot, bitter tears sprang to Tiana's eyes and anger flared in her belly so fiercely that she could hardly breathe just thinking about all that she had been through since her father's death. Drake touched her hand gently.

"I know you miss him, Tee, but you know wherever his soul went he is watching over you," Drake comforted her, giving her hand a reassuring squeeze.

Tiana closed her eyes and inhaled. Her father's face played out on the backs of her eyelids for a few quick seconds; that infectious smile that Tiana loved so much brought back so many good feelings. She could no longer hold back another round of tears as they fell in streams down her cheeks.

"You ready to do this?" Drake asked as his car slowed to a stop in the leaf-littered circular driveway.

"Yeah, but I need to go in alone," Tiana rasped, her mouth cotton-ball dry.

"Tee, let me go with—" Drake started.

"Drake." Tiana threw her hand up, halting his words. "I need to do this alone. I know he died in there. I know that memories of good and bad times are in there. I know all of that, but there is something I need to do, and I need to do it alone," Tiana said softly but firmly enough for Drake to understand.

He put his palms up in front of him and his eyebrows went into arches on his face. "Okay. Okay. If you say so. I'm out here waiting," Drake gave in, his expression letting her know he wouldn't protest any further.

"Thanks," Tiana replied, giving him a quick peck on the cheek. "That's why you my dude."

Tiana scrambled out of the car. Her legs were moving, but she didn't feel like she had control of them. Tiana wobbled and bobbed, looking like the Scarecrow from *The Wizard of Oz,* the result of every nerve in her body being alive and either pulsing or jittering.

Tiana kicked through the piles of dead leaves and tree branches that littered the porch. She inhaled deeply and slowly turned the knob on the front door. Surprisingly, the lock clicked, and the door creaked open. A tornado of emotion swirled around Tiana and her heart galloped. As she stepped inside, the terror she was feeling suddenly congealed into a sizzling ball of fury.

"They fucking shot you down like a dog in your own home, *Papi.* They won't get away with it," Tiana said through her teeth. Her anger propelled her forward, and the cold, empty, hollow, abandoned house no longer scared her. Tiana navigated through the expansive property like she still lived there. She rounded corners and descended steps like she had come home to stay. When she made it to the basement, she waved her hands in front of her face and swept away several thick tangles of spider webs. The basement was dank and dark except for a small rectangle of light coming from the tiny ground-level window.

Standing at the end of the steps for a few seconds, Tiana could still picture the pool table that used to sit in the center of the room. It was a big hit with her father's coworkers, who would crowd around throwing money down, placing bets on games. The pool table was often the instigator of a lot of friendly disputes among the guys.

Tiana turned to her left where the tall *Ms. Pac-Man* arcade game used to sit. It was her father's favorite game. He once told Tiana that when he was a kid, they didn't have video games in the house; they had to go to the arcade and pay a quarter to play the big stand-up games. So, when her father purchased the house he had bought the actual arcade game, too.

Tiana smiled now, thinking about the time she had beat her father at *Ms. Pac-Man*. "Pay up, *Papi*. You owe me now. You said nobody in the world could beat you," Tiana had demanded playfully, extending her open palm. Her father had gone into his pocket and slammed a one-hundred-dollar bill into the palm of her hand.

"Damn, *mija,* you ain't going to give your old man a break," her father had said, laughing. Now that Tiana thought back, he had to have let her win.

Tiana didn't even realize how hard she was crying until she felt her shoulders quaking and her legs shaking. Sucking in nostrils full of snot, Tiana slowly walked over to the wall where her father's desk used to sit. She placed her hand up against the wall.

"Ten, nine, eight, seven, six, five, four . . ." Tiana counted down, pressing her hand against the wall with each count.

"One," Tiana huffed. The wall was a tad softer at that spot, just like she remembered.

Tiana used her foot to kick the spot. The first kick didn't even dent the wall. Tiana huffed and grunted. This time she reared back and shot her foot forward with so much force pain shot from her foot all the way up to her pelvis. Plaster and paint crumbled to the floor. Tiana kicked the wall again but, this time, she turned around, bent her leg at the knee, and backed the bottom of her foot into the wall. The kick was more effective than any of the others. The wall gave way.

Tiana turned toward the hole, bent down, and used her hands to dig away the remaining plaster. She spotted the long black bag behind the wall and suddenly felt like she didn't have enough strength to keep digging. Tiana sucked in her breath and raised her hands to her neck as she felt like she was being choked by the memory that invaded her mind.

The Caldoron Home
Four Years Earlier

"What is it, Papi? What's the surprise?" Tiana asked excitedly as she followed her father down the stairs to the area of the house that he used for his office. It was where he held meetings with businessmen and hung out with his crew, the Los Asesinos, a crew of hired hit men.

"Shhh, mija. I don't want your stepmother to hear. This has to stay between just us," her father shushed her. Tiana followed him, watching his long jet-black ponytail swing at his back with every smooth step he took.

Tiana's father walked to a far wall a few steps from his custom mahogany desk. She watched him with her face crinkled in confusion as he bent down, pulled a perfect square of sheetrock from the wall, and set it aside.

"Ven aca," he summoned her. Tiana walked to her father's side and bent down in front of the opening in the wall.

"Everything I've been teaching you is for your own good. I don't want you to be like me when you grow up, but I want you to be able to protect yourself," her father said seriously.

Tiana nodded. He had given her this same speech many times before. She knew her father was hired to kill people and he knew that she was aware of what he did. He had spent years showing her how to think like a trained killer, but he had also made it clear that he never wanted her to be a killer for hire.

"So, this is for you if you ever need it," he said, pulling a long military-style Blackhawk bag from the wall.

Tiana's eyebrows went into arches on her face, and she held her breath as her father unzipped the bag. Wide-eyed, she looked at the contents of the bag and then looked up at her father and back down into the bag.

"This is called a war bag. If ever you have to go to war to protect yourself or your family, this will be here. Our secret," her father assured her, handing her a beautiful .40-caliber Glock with a shiny silver handle. The gun was almost too big for her hands. "This I had made just for you. You remember how we practiced shooting the forty, right?"

Tiana nodded.

"Very good. Your protection is right here. Our secret."

She watched her father stuff the black bag back into the opening in the wall. He put the piece of sheetrock back up to the opening in the wall and got to his feet.

"Tomorrow when you come down here you won't see this hole. It will be all closed up and painted. Here is how you find it when you need it," her father said, walking away from the cutout in the wall. Tiana watched him *with rapt attention as he walked to the opposite corner of the wall.*

"One, two, three, four," he counted until he was stand-ing at the wall behind his desk. "It's ten steps from the end of the wall to the spot. That won't change. Now you try," he told her.

Tiana did as she was told, moving her hand along the wall just slightly. It was a perfect ten when she reached the cutout in the wall.

"Good. You found the spot," her father complimented her, kissing the top of her head. "I will always try to be here so that you never need that war bag," he said as he wrapped his arms around her and gave her a warm hug. "But just in case something happens to me—"

"Nothing will happen to you. I love you, Papi," Tiana cooed, squeezing her father as hard as she could.

Tiana blinked away the tears and the memories. She forcefully tugged on the bag until she pulled it through the hole. She coughed from the white cloud of plaster dust that blew into her face. Without bothering to brush the dust from the top of the bag, Tiana unzipped it. She parted a sly smile when she saw that the contents were just as she had remembered: a .40-caliber Glock 23 with a customized silver handle, a .357 Sig Sauer with a black slip-proof rubber grip, two silencers, and her father's collections of six stainless steel hunting knives that varied in size.

In another small compartment on the front of the bag, Tiana found two rubber-banded stacks of money. Her father hadn't mentioned anything about leaving money in the bag for her, but she sure was grateful for it. She didn't have time to count it now, but she was sure it was enough to help her get some things she needed and to also help her carry out some of her plans.

"Thank you, *Papi*. I promise I won't let you down," Tiana whispered, hoisting the bag onto her shoulder and rushing toward the basement stairs.

Tiana hurried straight to the trunk of Drake's car and knocked on it. He had been so engrossed in a phone conversation he hadn't even seen Tiana exit the house. He waved, acknowledging her, and used the automatic button to pop the trunk for her. Once her bag was in the trunk, Tiana jumped into the car.

"You good?" Drake asked, one eyebrow raised.

"Yeah, you know me," Tiana replied. "I take it on the chin and bounce right back, Drake."

"That's what I like to hear." He smiled. "Listen, Tee, I gotta drop you to the apartment that I got set up for you. Sorry I can't hang out tonight. Some shit is going down on the street, and I gotta make an appearance," Drake told her.

"What's up?" Tiana quizzed.

"Somebody made a hit on my boss's family," Drake said, shaking his head in disgust. "It was some real horrible shit. He's out for blood, and he's making all his distributors have a roundtable meeting. His loyal soldiers are trying to figure out if we are at war. The hit came out of nowhere. There will definitely be bloodshed behind this shit. I might have to get my hands dirty this time. Somebody killed the heir to the throne so I'ma take this opportunity to show my boss I'm loyal and down for my peoples. If he sees how I do my work and take care of shit, you might be looking at the next prince of the streets. I'm about to blow up!"

Tiana swallowed hard and tried to keep her heart from coming up out of her mouth. Suddenly she was thinking about the explosion and how fast everything had happened. It was her first real kill, and she still felt good to think that Dr. Syed was dead but she couldn't stop thinking about that innocent little kid who was murdered along with him.

Tiana snapped out of her thoughts. "Well, you be careful, Drake. I'd be fucked up if something happened to you."

"Yeah, this shit is not a game right now. S. Gates ain't no fuck boy. We talking about one of the most dangerous motherfuckers in the game," Drake said with feeling. "He's going to fucking torture whoever is responsible before he kills them and their entire family. He is nothing to fuck with, and he has major connections all over the city. He's pissed as all hell and he ain't gonna stop until he finds the people who murked his son. The streets about to be lit like a motherfucker."

Chapter 10

"Help me! Oh, God, help me!" Manuelo bawled, the veins in his face and neck cording at the surface of his skin. Blood mixed with his tears made a mess all over his face, neck, and chest. His legs trembled, and his teeth chattered.

"Oh, Manny, God can't help you right now, my friend." Eric chortled as he circled Manuelo like a buzzard over a carcass. "Only you can help yourself right now, Manny. Only you."

"Ah, I told you everything I know," Manuelo cried, his chin falling to his chest. He was exhausted. It had been six hours since he'd been snatched from his bed in the middle of the night. It had been five and half hours that he'd endured Eric's torture.

"I'ma ask you one more time. Who ordered the hit on Gates's family?" Eric growled, his two large gold teeth glinting at Manuelo like evil eyes. Eric had been S. Gates's number one enforcer for eight years and so far he had a 100 percent confession rate.

"I . . . I swear I don't—" Manuelo cried, but he never got to finish. "Agh!" Manuelo howled, his words tumbling back down his throat like hard marbles when Eric cut a deep gash into the skin and muscle of his left bicep this time.

"C'mon, I hate to do this to you, but I need the answer. Who ordered the hit?" Eric was relentless. He was going to get something out of Manny one way or another.

Manuelo shook his head left to right. "Agh!" he squealed again, this time because Eric twisted the knife in circles, digging farther into his arm muscle.

Eric let out an exasperated breath and stood up. He stepped back a few paces and examined the mess of a man in front of him. He turned his head to the side and spit on the floor next to Manuelo. "You playing tough, huh?" Eric grumbled. He turned around and grabbed a box of iodized salt from the small metal table behind him and smiled evilly.

"Now, Manny. Be a good little boy and tell me if it was Los Diablos who sent the bomb that killed that little boy," Eric snarled, shaking the box of salt menacingly. "He was my boss's only son. He was the next in line to take over the business. Which means somebody is going to die over this for sure."

"I don't know about a hit." Manuelo panted out each word, drool leaking from his lips.

"You are just so fucking loyal, aren't you!" Eric barked, his eyes hooding over with malice. With that, Eric emptied the entire box of salt into the open wounds covering Manuelo's body, taking time to crush some of the salt down into the huge, gaping holes on Manuelo's right thigh.

"Agh! Jesus Christ!" Manuelo squealed, his body bucking so fiercely against the chair and restraints that the chains binding him cut farther into his skin.

Unfazed, Eric moved close to Manuelo's downturned head so that he could whisper in his ear. "Tell your boss that S. Gates will keep taking his men one by one until he finds out who killed his son and his brother. The only reason you live today is to send the message; but next time, a Diablos dies. Consider yourself lucky to be alive," Eric hissed like a venomous snake. Manuelo hung his head in so much pain he wished for death.

S. Gates stood behind the double-sided mirror watching Eric inflict torture on one of his rival's men. Gates hadn't taken his eyes off of Manuelo, one of René Rodriguez's top earners among the Diablos.

S. Gates took great satisfaction in watching the pain and suffering in the man's eyes and hearing his screams. It was all he could do to console himself after the loss of his brother and son. S. Gates couldn't believe his little boy was gone forever. He lived for his son, and everything he did was for him. Now that he was gone, S. Gates's number one priority was to avenge his son's death. He didn't care how many enemies he made or how many lives he had to take until he found his son's killer.

He knew torturing the Los Diablos men would thrust him and his crew into a war once it got back to René, but he had nothing left to lose so he couldn't care less what happened from here. He was also feeling the loss of his bother Peter. It was messed up they used him to get to his son.

Peter had always told him to leave him out of all the dirty shit that went down with his crew. When Gates first started running and learning the ropes in the streets, Peter tried to get him to stay focused on getting good grades in school and getting a scholarship to college. But he was never book smart. He had a business mind but not the kind that'd have you sitting behind a desk dealing with paperwork for the rest of your life. The brothers were completely different. Peter ended up going to medical school while Gates stayed in the streets and built his crew. It was blood and street money that paid for Peter's education. But now Gates felt guilty that his brother paid the ultimate price.

"Boss?"

The voice interrupted S. Gates's thoughts. Something he hated. S. Gates turned around slowly and ice-grilled Blaine, one of his workers.

"I just got back from seeing our contact at the police department, and he gave me these to give you," Blaine rushed his words out, extending a large manila envelope toward S. Gates. "It's from their investigation into the explosion, but he said he thought you would want to see them right away. In case you wanted to take on the job before they do."

Gates took the envelope, turned it over, and dumped the contents into his hand. He squinted his eyes as he examined the large, eight-by-ten glossy photographs.

"What is this?" S. Gates asked, his jaw going stiff and his eyebrows dipping on his face.

"Those are the images from the security cameras outside of your brother's house. It was dark but, as you can see from these, it doesn't look like it was men who put the explosives in the car. The cops are thinking it was two women, from the profiles they see here. The hoods make it hard to see the faces, but you can clearly see breasts on one of them, and you can see ass on both," Blaine explained. He walked closer to S. Gates and extended his hand, "May I?" he asked.

Gates nodded, handing Blaine the stack of pictures. He loosened his tie and flexed his neck. Suddenly his expensive Brooks Brothers suit and custom-tailored dress shirt felt too small and too scratchy against his skin.

"In this one, you can see a partial face. Like I said, it was dark and the pictures are grainy, but it's a start. I'd say it looks like a female for sure," Blaine said, handing his boss one of the pictures. He studied the picture closely, his nostrils flaring.

"So if it was the Diablos who sent the hit, either they are hiring women now, or we got the wrong clues about who carried out that hit and we went after the wrong people."

"Yeah, I was thinking the same thing, boss. I was even starting to think maybe this didn't have anything to do with Los Diablos at all," Blaine continued, treading lightly with his next words. "It could be possible we went after the wrong people. Did your brother have enemies or was he into any weird shit?"

Gates considered what Blaine was telling him. If they had gone in under the wrong assumptions, it was too late to go back on it now. As far as considering if this had something to do with his brother, Gates highly doubted it did. His brother was quiet guy and didn't have issues with anyone as far as he knew. Peter was all about his job at Rollins. Often times Gates would tease him and ask him if he had a side chick in there because he seemed to spend more time at the facility than he did at home with his wife.

He stood, brooding, his chest rising and falling rapidly. He turned back toward the double-sided mirror and glanced out at the bruised, bleeding, half-dead victim on the other side. Gates didn't allow a lot of people to know who he was in the streets, but those who did get to be in his presence knew that he had a short fuse and a penchant for extreme violence when the situation called for it.

"No matter what those pictures say and who we think carried out the hit, the fact remains we are at war with somebody," he said evenly. "Make sure my wife doesn't get wind of those pictures. She is still convinced it was faulty wires in the car that caused the explosion and that's the way I want it to stay. She's been through enough already."

Chapter 11

A few days had passed since Cee Cee had returned home. It was crazy to think that she felt like stranger in the house she grew up in. After the initial encounter between her and her mother, they hadn't exchanged many words. She purposely avoided Marie and mostly stayed in her room. She was pleasantly surprised to learn that her room hadn't been turned into a guest room and that her things were still there exactly as she'd left them. Maybe her mother did have a little love for her after all.

"Good morning, Sleeping Beauty."

She heard a voice coming from behind her. She spun around to see Vinny standing in the doorway of the kitchen. She had come down to grab some cereal for breakfast. "Good morning."

"So you do come out of your room."

"I come out when I need to," she replied.

He got straight to the point. "So, what's your problem with me and your mother? You know I always cared about you two."

"My problem with you and my problem with her are two different things," she began to explain as she carried her bowl of cereal to the kitchen table and took a seat.

"Go on," he said as he followed her. He sat in the chair directly across from her.

"My problem with you is that you left my father to die the night he was killed. From what I was told, you were standing right next to him when he was stabbed and, instead of helping him get to the car, you ran off and just left him there stabbed up and hurt like that. He was your best friend, Vinny, and like a coward when shit hit the fan you abandoned him and left him there to bleed out and die. He had nobody there with him when he took his last breath."

"I don't have to explain shit to you about the night your dad died," Vinny responded as he looked her square in the eyes.

"No, you don't, because there is nothing you can say to me that is going to change anything anyway," she agreed with him. For a good thirty seconds, they just sat there staring each other down, neither of them breaking contact or blinking.

Vinny finally broke the silence. "Explain the situation with your mother." His facial expression seemed dark and cold.

"My mother is a sneaky, weak bitch with no loyalty," she said with no emotion whatsoever. "She knew exactly what she was doing when she got the doctor to prescribe all those antidepressant and anxiety pills. She knew I wasn't doing well and she purposely kept talking to me about overdoses and shit like that. It's like she wanted me to kill myself. Then she has me locked up in the psych ward and ends up fucking you and moving you into our house. I will never respect that."

"So if you hate me and you mother so much then why the fuck are you here?" he asked.

"I came by because I need work. I want to do a few jobs so I can make some money for myself," Celeste said pointedly, now finishing up her breakfast. She looked at Vinny to see if she could read him and get a feel for what was going through his mind.

He threw his head back and laughed raucously. "Work? You putting in work now?"

"Yeah, I am, and I'm probably better than all these clowns you got working for you and you know it. I learned from the best; or did you forget that my father started teaching me the ropes from when I was fifteen?" Cee Cee retorted, glaring at Vinny to put emphasis on her words. She wanted to make sure to remind him of her close relationship with her father.

"How could I forget?" he said as more of a statement than a question.

"He wanted me to learn everything so I could eventually take over," she went on. "But, now that he's gone, I see you have stepped in and have basically replaced him in everything."

As if on cue, just as she finished her last statement her mother walked into the room. "Morning," she said nonchalantly, not realizing she had just walked in on a very serious conversation. "What are you two talking about?"

"Oh, nothing," Cee Cee replied just as nonchalantly as her mother. "We were just talking about how Vinny is trying to replace Dad and seems to want to pretend he's him. He sure as hell fooled you since you got him living in here running shit," Cee Cee said and started laughing sarcastically.

"Listen, Celeste, you will respect me as long as you're in this house."

"Oh, I know you're not talking about respect, Mom. You have no idea what the meaning of that word is. Look how you're disrespecting Dad's memory by having Vinny be all up in this house like he owns it."

"Okay, I've had enough of your shit," Vinny snapped. "I worked with your dad half of my life. I ain't trying to replace or pretend to be nobody. I know who the fuck I am. I will never forget Louis. He saved me from the streets when I was young, and he took me in and let me come into the business when he didn't have to. He treated me like a son, and I won't ever forget that," Vinny said, his voice going low. He hated when he talked about Louis like that. He hated when people compared him to Louis or reminded him that Louis was responsible for his rise. "What I'm doing here is keeping his dream alive. Handling his business to keep his memory going," he stated with pride.

"Well, in his memory, give me a chance to prove myself," Tiana said.

"Prove yourself doing what?" Marie quizzed.

"I want to prove that Daddy taught me well on how to get paid from people. I wanna prove that I can make my own money. I wanna get an apartment and take care of myself. I'm not trying to live off nobody else. I can put in work just like anybody. Plus, nobody will see me coming, unlike those gorilla goons you got working for you who are probably like bulls in a china shop."

"A'ight, let me see what I can arrange," Vinny said as the wheels in his head began spinning.

"Wait one fucking minute," Marie said, trying to voice her opinion. "I don't want you out there—"

"Marie! Leave and let me speak to Celeste!" Vinny snapped. "Get the fuck outta here!" he exclaimed, waving his hand at Marie dismissively.

Cee Cee felt a warm twinge of satisfaction in her chest as she saw the hurt register on her mother's face. She smirked, watching her mother turn and walk out of the kitchen. She made her way up the stairs without saying another word like a scolded child.

Weak bitch, Cee Cee said in her head.

"So, let me talk to you in my office." Vinny grinned as he walked out of the kitchen and made his way down the hallway to his office in the back room of the first floor, with Cee Cee following.

It used to be Louis's office, but it had undergone a major renovation since Vinny took it over. Louis used to have dark burgundy on the walls and liked large, bulky, handcrafted wooden furniture. Vinny had different tastes. He loved light colors and preferred sleek and edgy furniture. When he took the office over, the first thing he did was replace that dark color on the wall with a light gray and white honeycomb wallpaper. He put a glass-top dark tinted desk with charcoal metal legs and a black leather chair on one end of the room. On the desk, all he had was his silver HP desktop.

On the other side of the office, he had a wet bar installed. He kept the wet bar stocked with only top-shelf liquors. Directly across from the wet bar he put two gray tufted chairs and a small gray love seat. A black coffee table with silver encrusted coasters stood in the middle of the chairs and love seat. The floor-to-ceiling windows that overlooked the greenery in the backyard were covered with mustard yellow curtains. The color of the curtains gave the room a perfect balance of colors.

Vinny walked into his office and took a seat on the love seat. Once he was comfortable, he turned his attention back to Cee Cee. He patted a place next to him on his gray microfiber couch. Cee Cee sat down, but not as close as Vinny had summoned her.

"I don't bite," he said, urging her closer. "You wanted to talk business, right?" he said, giving her a large, wide smile to reveal his pearly whites.

Cee Cee moved a few inches closer to him, convincing herself to just go along with him so she could get him to give her an assignment. The closer she got to Vinny, the stronger the scent of his Platinum Chanel cologne became. It was the scent Dr. Syed always wore, so the fact that Vinny was wearing it made Cee Cee's stomach churn.

"I always thought you were beautiful, Celeste. More beautiful than Marie or any other woman I know," Vinny whispered, touching Cee Cee's hair softly.

Cee Cee scrunched her face and snaked her head away from his hands. This wasn't what she was expecting.

"You know, all of this was meant for you to have. That's the way Louis always wanted it. A young guy like me should have a young woman like you as my queen," Vinny said seductively, his hand moving to Cee Cee's thigh. The hairs all over her body stood up, and she balled her toes up in her sneakers.

"I stayed with her because I felt sorry for her after Louis died," Vinny continued, nodding toward the front of the house. "I never felt for her like I always felt for you. I was just waiting for you to grow up. I always wanted you for myself. You're so much smarter. You deserve to be the queen."

Celeste was twelve when her father came home with Vinny. Vinny was six years older than her. She was just a kid when they had first met. As the years went on and Vinny saw how she was filling out, he became attracted to her. Now that she was nineteen and her father wasn't around anymore, it was the perfect time for him to make his move.

"What?" Cee Cee snapped. "You're fucking my mother, and you think I would fuck you too?" She gasped in disbelief. If eyes could kill Vinny would've died on the spot from the sharp glares she shot his way.

"No. You misunderstand. I don't want you both at the same time, Celeste. I will get rid of her if I can have you. She won't suffer. I know she's fucking weak, so I won't turn her out with nothing. I will put her up and make sure she's taken care of if you come and sit by my side as my lady. You'll be the queen of the new crew. There's been a lot of changes since you been gone. We're not lending people money anymore. We're done with all that shit. I ain't got time to be chasing people for money they don't want to pay back," Vinny explained to her.

"I shook hands with some people and I partnered us up with the Diablos now," he revealed proudly. "So our job is to take out whoever they need us to take and make collections for them. We in a whole different ballgame now. You can have everything that I have. You have no idea for how long and how much I've wanted you. Things are different since Louis's been gone. I run a different type of business. More lucrative. More ruthless. I get more business than your father ever did because people know I don't care what the fuck is going on. I get money one way or another. Times changed so we had to change. The guys are happier. They're making more money than they did under your father's reign. You could still benefit from what should rightfully be yours, Celeste."

Cee Cee's skin crawled as she listened to Vinny. *My father must be turning over in his grave right now,* was all that ran through her mind listening to everything Vinny was telling her. *How could Mom just stand by and watch this happen?* At the same time, it was no surprise that her mother had just let everything go down the way it had. She never cared about anything but herself. As long as she had everything she needed to keep herself up, she couldn't care less about the details.

With Vinny taking over and teaming up with another crew, everything Louis stood for had probably gone to shit. Louis was old school with old school, old gangster philosophies, and although he was ruthless and killed a time or two he always believed in rules and order. Louis's number one rule was to not ever kill innocent women and children. It was for that reason that Cee Cee had been so upset about the kid who died in the explosion with Dr. Syed. She felt like she had gone against everything her father had taught her.

Cee Cee was pretty sure from hearing how Vinny was talking that he was running the crew as the complete opposite of how her father had run it. Vinny's new school crew had no rules, no charter, no morals, and for them it was money over everything, even if it meant women and children had to die in the crosshairs.

Cee Cee got to her feet, her face folded into a frown and her fists clenched at her sides. "I'm not looking to be nobody's queen. And I'm not interested in being a part of your new crew. If you say you are in charge of offing some of their rivals and collecting for them then just send a couple of assignments my way. I just want a few jobs so I can get on my feet. I'm not trying to be committed to nobody right now. I want to be independent. I have to get my life in order," she said proudly.

Vinny's smile dropped, and he clenched his hands into fists. He bit down into his jaw, and his eyes hooded over. Taking rejection wasn't his strong point. He thrived on power plays and aggression. "So you deny me? Just like that?" he asked.

"No. I will do jobs for you to get paid," Cee Cee clarified. "But I won't be your queen and be all wifed up with you," she said as she stood up from the couch.

"If I give you jobs what are you going to give me?" he asked, his jaw rocking and his head moving up and down.

"The best work for less money," Celeste replied. "If you pay your guys fifty stacks for a job, I'll do it for forty. I can do any job they can do and probably better."

"What other jobs can you do better?" Vinny asked, getting to his feet, and moving his body behind Cee Cee until she could feel his erection pressing on her ass. She felt the heat of his breath on her neck. "What else will you give me?" he breathed into her ear, his hands traveling to her breasts and his tongue touching her cheek. Cee Cee felt anger flaring in her belly and was about to push him off of her when her mother walked into the room.

"Celeste, why did you come here?" Marie's voice boomed from behind. Vinny jumped and quickly moved away from Cee Cee. "You came to take my man? Huh? To ruin my life all over again?" Marie spat, moving around Cee Cee like a lioness on the prowl. "It wasn't enough you stole your daddy from me when I had you; now you came here to try to steal my man again! You never wanted to see me happy! Did you? Did you?"

Cee Cee spun around to meet her mother eye to eye. Heat flared in Cee Cee chest, and she got ready for war. "Fuck you and your man! I could have him if I wanted to. Lucky for you I don't want shit to do with him unless it's about work. That's what the fuck I came here for. I came here to get work." She was so furious she could feel her heart beating and the adrenaline running though her veins.

"I definitely didn't come to catch up with you and let you know how your only daughter was doing. It's not like you ever gave any fucks about me anyway. And how dare you think I stole Daddy from you? He was my fucking father. He loved me as his daughter and you as his wife. Do you honestly think I ever wanted to take your place with him? Fuck I want with your life? You ain't living; you just surviving, moving another man into this house. Lying on your back and spreading your legs and sucking some dick just to keep yourself feeling and looking good. I don't know how Dad ever saw anything in you. I'm ashamed to be your daughter. You ain't nothing more than a fuck and a suck to somebody. That's all you've ever been good for," Cee Cee hissed, fire flashing in her eyes.

The women stood toe to toe, both exuding palpable waves of fury. Vinny quickly wedged his body between them; and two of his goons who had overheard the commotion ran into the room and slid over to where they all stood.

"Okay. Okay. I have a small job for you. If you prove yourself, I will have more work for you, maybe even steady work," Vinny placated her, pushing Marie out of Cee Cee's reach. As much as he would have enjoyed a knock-down, drag-out mother and daughter fight, he had a meeting to get to so he had to leave soon.

"Nah, I'm not signing on to anybody's payroll. I'm just looking for a few quick independent jobs. I'm not joining your new crew," Cee Cee clarified.

Vinny looked at the fury in Cee Cee eyes and smirked. "We will see how long you survive out here without the backing of a crew," Vinny said, his ego clearly bruised from her constant rejection.

"I'll take my chances. Now, what's the job and how much does it pay?" Cee Cee replied, getting right down to business, feeling the heat of her mother's gaze on her face.

Chapter 12

Lost, lonely, and confused, Izzy had been aimlessly walking down Dort Highway for almost an hour. She couldn't believe that Shawn had moved on without her. She couldn't understand why her life had been so fucked up for her. Every time she thought things were going to get better, something worse would happen.

When she met Shawn, she thought God had finally answered her prayers and she had found her Prince Charming. They met at the strip club, and when he found out that she didn't have a place to stay, he moved her in to his apartment and things started to look up. She was still working her nightshifts at the club, but instead of working every night, she cut her schedule down to just four days a week. On her days off, she would clean the house, cook her man breakfast, lunch, and dinner, and sit with him while he played his beloved video games.

Shawn was the perfect boyfriend to her. He had a good, steady job, paid the bills all on his own, and seemed to genuinely enjoy spending time with her. After about three months of them living in bliss, things began to spiral out of control. He came home one morning and said he had gotten laid off. He seemed devastated to lose his job, and Izzy did her best to cheer him up and keep him in good spirits.

The first few weeks he was determined to find another job quickly. He updated his résumé and was out the door no later than ten in the morning to go to different places and fill out applications, and do interviews on the spot. He picked up odd jobs whenever he came across them and he signed up for online programs that offered to send him job alerts every week. At first he was getting e-mails and callbacks asking him to come in for interviews. He got a few job offers, but he turned them all down because they were all offering him less money than what he was making. Eventually, the phone stopped ringing and e-mails stopped coming in.

Elizabeth went back to working six days a week to pick up the slack and cover the bills. When Shawn realized that she was bringing in more than he was before he got fired, he stopped looking for work. He started going out with his friends, hanging out at bars, and spending money as fast as Izzy was making it. Izzy didn't mind stepping up and helping out with everything if it weren't for the fact that Shawn was still expecting her to cook, clean, and take care of everything in the house when she got off work in the morning.

She would get home around four in the morning and usually find the apartment a mess with bottles thrown about and cigarettes put out everywhere. Shawn and his friends would be passed out in different places throughout the apartment. Instead of going to bed to get some rest, Izzy would immediately get to cleaning up behind everyone because she knew in the morning Shawn would be up and expecting the apartment to look spotless and his breakfast to be cooking on the stove.

When Izzy tried asking him if there was any news on him getting a new job, he would flip out on her and accuse her of being a gold-digging whore. He would tell her that the only reason she was so anxious for him to get a job was because she was fucking different guys while he was at work because that's all strippers were good for. When she tried reassuring him that it wasn't true, he became more infuriated and accused her of calling him a liar. There was no winning with him and nothing Izzy did was ever good enough for him.

Eventually, screaming and putting her down was not enough for him and he began to beat on her for any reason he could think of. Despite all of the abuse, Izzy never thought of leaving him because he was all she had. She didn't have any friends, and she loved him. After every beating, she would convince herself that it was her fault he did what he did. She would go and apologize to him for fear that he would stay mad at her if she didn't.

Izzy was tired of walking along the highway. She was in a daze, confused about what she was going to do next. She was considering going into Déjà Vu and seeing if she could start working some night shifts again but being that she had been gone for so long, she didn't know if they'd take her back just like that. When she went into the ward, she asked them repeatedly if she could call her job so she could let them know that she was going to have to take a leave, but they never allowed her to use the phone. She had a feeling that if she showed up after all this time, they'd be mad at her for not showing up or calling.

Izzy pulled at the wedgie she had from wearing Laura's pants. She must have been a petite girl because these pants Izzy had on were a full size too small for her. Izzy wondered if Laura was prettier than her. She wondered how Laura and Shawn had met and how long it had been before Shawn moved her in. The more she thought about the situation, the more infuriated she became.

She had gone through hell at that psych ward getting raped by Dr. Syed and his staff. She had been drugged, sodomized, and abused in that hospital and, all that time, what got her through was thinking about getting back to Shawn. She had taken beating after beating, and all she thought about was Shawn. And to think that entire time she was suffering Shawn was out here moving on and loving someone else. Izzy started to feel a passion from deep within that she had never felt before. It was like she was waking up for the first time and seeing things for what they really were.

Tiana and Cee Cee kept telling her to stop thinking about Shawn and to just focus on getting herself better. They warned her about going back to him and told her that she could do better. They told her that he was an asshole for beating her and taking advantage of her like that. She never told them but there were some days that Shawn even made her strip for his friends and one time even made her sleep with one of them.

Shawn told her that if she loved him she would sleep with Mike, his best friend, because Shawn wanted Mike to see how good her pussy felt. She didn't feel comfortable doing it, but she did because she would do anything for Shawn. He was pissed off at her for giving away her body even though he asked her to and Shawn didn't touch her for a month. Izzy missed her period while she was waiting for Shawn to get over himself and she found out that she was pregnant with what was likely his friend's baby. Shawn then forced her to go to some hack job abortion clinic to get rid of it.

Now she understood what they all saw. She realized that Shawn was just using her and that he never really loved her. All that time, she meant nothing to him. *It's time for me to show him what I'm made of,* she said to herself. With that, she began the walk back toward his apartment.

By the time Izzy got to the apartment she was in a full rage thinking about all the fucked-up things Shawn put her through over the years. "How can this nigga treat me like this?" she ranted to herself. "I gave the best of myself to him and he just tossed me to the side like I was trash to him! Wait until I see this motherfucker; and his bitch better not be in there 'cause she can get it too," she mumbled to herself as she walked up the steps.

Izzy stood in front of the door with her chest heaving in and out like she had just finished running a marathon. Just as she was about to knock, she paused and heard laughter on the other side. That was all the fuel she needed to increase the fire that was burning within her.

Shawn was sitting at the dinner table with Laura reminiscing about the last time they had sex at her job and how they were almost caught by the floor manager. "If you saw your face when you heard the door unlock, you would've thought you got caught with your pants down. Wait, you almost did!" Shawn roared out with a hearty laugh.

"Well, if you hadn't insisted on nutting on my face while I had my makeup on I never would've yelled out. Oh my God, imagine if you had nutted on my face. How the fuck would I have ever explained that shit to my manager?" Laura said in a matter-of-fact tone, as she didn't find it so funny.

"You know how: tell that motherfucker it was a glazed bear claw you got smacked with." Shawn couldn't help himself from busting out laughing at his corny jokes.

Laura wasn't pleased being the butt of Shawn's jokes. But when she knew better than to say anything that would get him upset and cause him to start going off on her.

Shawn was still laughing at the thought of how funny it would've been if they had been caught by the manager when he heard a loud knocking coming from the front door. Boom, boom, boom, boom! If he didn't know any better he would of thought it was the feds with a battering ram looking for a drug bust.

This scared the shit out of Laura. She knew Shawn lived in the hood, but banging like that was never heard of where she was from.

Shawn reluctantly stood up to answer the door. What he really wanted to do was hop through the bathroom window and run just in case it really was the cops looking to cause some trouble. Them alphabet boys stayed making things worse than they were. It was bad enough with people struggling in poverty out there in Flint. With all the cop killing that had been going on all over, Shawn wasn't looking to be the next name on that list.

"Who's that?" he asked in a low but deep voice.

Boom, boom, boom, boom! Another round of banging came again, this time with a female's voice screaming behind it, "Open this fucking door, you trifling, bitch-ass nigga and find out who it is!"

Shawn was confused because he didn't recognized the voice.

"Who is that?" Laura mouthed without a sound to him.

Shawn shrugged and shook his head from side to side. He tried to peep through the side window but it was too dark to make out who it was. He was sure it wasn't the cops at this point because he didn't see flashing red and blue lights in front of the house when he peeped through the window.

He slowly opened the door. When he saw who it was he chuckled and completely let his guard down. Shawn pushed the door back to shut the door in her face. Just as Shawn motioned to close it, Izzy caught a glimpse of Laura for the first time. She darted right past Shawn, determined to choke out the bitch who had taken her man.

Shawn was taken aback by Izzy's actions and he didn't know how to react. Everything happened so fast. He saw as Izzy cocked her arm back and cold-clocked Laura right in the nose. Immediately Laura's nose started gushing as Izzy kept throwing haymakers in her direction.

He quickly ran toward them to break up Izzy's power-beating on Laura, who was now on the ground in the fetal position attempting to protect herself. What Shawn didn't realize was that Izzy was too far gone in her mind to be stopped by anything or anyone. Shawn came up from behind and attempted to get Izzy off of his girl.

All three of them were now in the small kitchen. Shawn managed to put Izzy in a full Nelson to get her off of Laura. After a few seconds Izzy eased off of fighting Shawn back and let him pull her up. Shawn was shocked when he looked down and saw the damage Izzy had done to Laura's face. He never knew Izzy had it in her to be so violent.

Izzy came to the realization that he had the nerve to defend that bitch over her. "Don't you know you're supposed to be mine!" Izzy yelled. "Everything I do is because of you. All I ever wanted was for you to be happy with me. But instead you beat me, put me down, and then went out and got some other bitch to take my place. I got sent up to Rollins because of all your fucking lies and I kept my mouth shut and never told them the truth. You have no idea all the shit they did to me while I was in there. They raped me and abused me night after night and it was because of you," Izzy yelled with tears streaming down her face and spit flying out of her mouth as she spoke. "Because of you!"

"What the fuck are you talking about?" Shawn yelled back, confused.

"You motherfucker. You! You're the reason I went to the psych ward. You're the reason I got hit by that car! You're the reason I was raped!" She began to weep. Her breathing had now become labored and she struggled to get those last words out. She was finding it harder and harder to catch a full breath and her knees started to buckle. When her legs finally gave way and she was about to fall, Shawn slapped her across the face.

"Bitch, you brave enough to run up in my house and act a fool! I'ma kill you for real this time."

Shawn's slap actually helped her get herself together again. It was like the slap made her catch her breath and forced the adrenaline to start coursing through her veins.

Shawn cocked his arm all the way back to give her a final backhanded pimp slap. As Shawn's hand was coming down Izzy mustered up all her energy to get up and push him across the kitchen floor. She felt the rage resurface in her. She searched around the room to use something to protect herself with. She saw the butcher knife sitting on the counter and snatched it up. Not knowing how to use it against him she pointed it in his direction. "Come on, bitch-ass nigga I'm sick of the bullshit of men touching my body when I don't want it!"

Shawn had slammed his head on the edge of the countertop. The hard blow to the head had him a bit confused about what had just happened. He knew he had fallen, but he was finding it hard to believe it was Izzy who had pushed him with such strong force.

He stumbled up from the floor to get his bearings. "I know you didn't just put your hands on me. I just told you, now you about to die," he said, applying pressure to the knot that was forming on his forehead. He was still talking the talk, but he was so dazed he was barely standing up straight. Izzy kept swinging the knife from left to right to get him to keep his distance. It didn't stop him from lunging toward her.

As he jumped forward, Izzy sliced the brachial artery on his left arm. "I told you I'm sick of you men touching me."

Shawn had no idea the arteries in his biceps were just as important as his carotid artery in his neck. Blood started gushing out of his arm within seconds. Izzy calmly walked over to the dining room table and took a seat.

By now Laura had managed to sit up and crawl over to Shawn, who was now sitting on the floor too. There was so much blood she couldn't make out where it was all coming from.

"Baby, you . . . you're . . . Shawn! Shawn! You're bleeding!" she screamed in a panic. "You hurt him!" Laura spat at Izzy.

"Yes, I did. Fuck around and you're next!" Izzy spat back.

"Ha! Who's next? Remember whose house this . . ." Shawn's voice trailed off. Even though he could barely move, he was still trying to get the last word in. "Fuck. I'm starting to . . . feel weak." Shawn passed out.

"Shawn!" Laura screamed, hoping to see a glimmer of life still in him. "Baby, baby, look at me. No, no, no, no," she said, frightened. "Hang on, baby. I'm gonna call the police."

"No, the fuck you not calling any police while I'm still here," Izzy said in a rage.

Laura had no idea who this girl was, but she wasn't trying to stick around and find out. She whispered a final, "I love you," to Shawn and then mustered up all the courage to crawl past Izzy so she could try to make a run for the door.

"Where the fuck do you think you're going?" Izzy grabbed her by the hair.

"Arg! Please, stop!" Laura pleaded. "Let me go. I promise I won't tell anybody about anything that happened," Laura tried to reason with her.

"You damn right you won't tell anybody about what happened." Izzy pulled her head back and made a swift cut across Laura's neck. She released her and watched as Laura began to grab at her neck to try to stop the blood from seeping out.

Izzy took a seat back at the dining room table still holding the knife in her hand. She sat there in silence just staring at the wall and rocking back and forth for what seemed like an eternity. Suddenly, a phone began to ring. Izzy snapped out of her trance and looked down at the bloody knife in her hands. She looked over to the kitchen and saw Shawn's and Laura's dead bodies.

She dropped the knife as if it were hot coal in her hands. She had wanted to confront Shawn and teach him a lesson, but a double homicide had never been part of the idea. She jumped up toward Shawn and picked up his lifeless body. She caressed his face and started to remember the good times they had together. Weeping, she turned his face toward her.

"I'm sorry, baby. All I wanted was you. Not money, not a home, not even kids. Just you." She looked at the knife on the floor. "Funny how you had them send me to the psych ward and they thought I was crazy." She laughed. "Well, they were right. I'm crazy for you, baby. And, now that you're gone, there's no point for me to live without you," she said as she reached over and grabbed the knife. She took a deep breath and sliced her wrists lengthwise. Izzy started bleeding out and she fell over. She landed right in between Laura and Shawn. She turned her head toward Laura.

"Laura, I know it wasn't your fault that he chose you, but he's . . . I'm getting tired," she said as everything started to go dark. "Fuck you, bitch."

Chapter 13

Cee Cee saw her marks as they made their way toward the address Vinny had given her. The way the man and woman scurried down the block, whipping their heads around like two paranoid schizophrenics, Cee Cee knew right away that they were fiends on the move and most likely high or chasing their next high.

Vinny had told Cee Cee that the dude, Pito, and his girlfriend, Linda, had stolen three kilos of cocaine from a drug kingpin named Preme. Preme had contracted Vinny to either get the drugs they'd stolen from him or to take care of the thieving couple. Vinny told Cee Cee she would get half of what the contract was worth if she carried out the job, but that he needed pictures as proof. She figured a double hit would net her at least forty stacks. She wasn't stupid; she knew how well kingpins paid for these types of revenge hits.

Cee Cee pulled her hood over her head and spread her fingers into the black leather gloves she had retrieved from her back pocket. She counted down in her head and, just as the fiends made it to their building door, Cee Cee made her move.

Pito jumped when he noticed Cee Cee standing right in front of him. "Damn, ma, you scared me," Pito huffed. It was like Cee Cee had just materialized out of the walls. Cee Cee smirked at him. He had no idea.

"Excuse me. Ladies first." Pito smiled at her, holding the door open so that his girlfriend and Cee Cee could enter.

She nodded her thanks. *Oh, a thief with manners,* Cee Cee said to herself.

Linda tapped on the elevator button, bouncing on her legs like she had to pee. Cee Cee took a good look at her and could tell Linda probably was a real beauty before the drugs had ravaged her skin, hair, teeth, and curves. Pito looked terrible too but, unlike his girlfriend, his clothes were neat, clean, and all high-end labels. His hair cut was sharp and he wore a gold pinky ring on his left hand. Cee Cee stood back and watched the pair. They both were jonesing bad for the drugs, but Linda showed the worst signs of needing a hit.

"Keep the fuck still," Pito cursed at Linda. "You making me fucking nervous. You look like a fucking crazy person moving all around like you got ants in your pants. Gotdamn!"

"Shut the fuck up! Don't tell me what to do, Pito. Shit, I'm fucked up right now. My nerves are fucked up and it's all because of you. Be a real man for a change and stop depending on me," Linda snapped, rubbing her arms and sniffling back the invisible snot she felt was coming out of her nose.

"Yeah, a'ight, bitch. You don't be making moves like I do. You sick right now because you don't listen," Pito shot back.

"No, you don't listen, motherfucker. I always get us right, even if I have to sell my ass. Bitch-ass nigga," Linda retorted, rolling her neck and getting close to Pito's face.

"Oh, you feeling real brave right now 'cause it's somebody else here right now. You just fucking wait 'til we get there," Pito threatened.

The elevator door opened, a welcome distraction from their back-and-forth bickering. Again, Pito allowed Cee Cee and Linda inside first. The shouting back and forth continued and took Pito's and Linda's attention off of Cee Cee.

Cee Cee went straight to the back wall of the small project elevator. She slid her hand to the gun Vinny had given her. Her stomach did flips and her chest moved up and down like she'd just finished running: a mixture of nerves, adrenaline, and anticipation. Pito and Linda stood close to the door with their backs to Cee Cee. Pito went to the corner opposite the elevator buttons and Linda stood right in front of the buttons, still dancing like she had a painfully full bladder.

Cee Cee watched Linda press the number nine button about fifteen times.

"You think if you press that shit a hundred times the elevator going to move any faster?" Pito snapped. "That fucking sound is really getting to me, so stop!"

"Shut the fuck up, Pito. For real, I'm in no mood for your shit. Acting like a bitch ass all the time," Linda barked back.

Cee Cee took a deep breath, curled her hand around her Glock with the silencer already screwed on, and eased it out. The couple was so engrossed in their argument that they never saw what was coming. Cee Cee slowly lifted her head and raised her arm at the same time. "Yo," she said, "Preme sent me for you. Where are the drugs?"

Linda and Pito both looked at her with fear written all over their faces.

"We didn't take nothing, I swear," Linda blurted out.

"Look, I don't know what the story is, and I don't give two shits about what the truth is. I came to collect three kilos. Now either you have it, or you don't."

"What are you gonna do if we don't have it?" Pito challenged her.

"I ain't gonna do shit," Cee Cee responded. "But my girl Lucy's gonna fuck you up."

"Who's Lucy?" he asked.

"This is Lucy." Cee Cee rushed the words out. She raised her gun swiftly and tugged back on the trigger. Pito threw his hands up, but it was too late. He took two bullets to his right temple and his body deflated to the floor like a balloon with the air let out of it. Linda let out an ear-shattering scream, turning toward Cee Cee with horror etched on her face.

"Please! No!" Linda screamed. She stumbled backward into the elevator's buttons, and the alarm sounded.

"Fuck!" Cee Cee huffed. Her hands shook so badly her gun wavered unsteadily in front of her. She tugged back on the trigger unsteadily, and the gun reared up in her hand. One bullet hit Linda in the cheek and the other in the forehead, causing her body to do an awkward pirouette and fall forward, blocking the elevator door. Cee Cee was covered with sweat; and the strong, raw meat odor of the blood almost made her throw up. Except for when she and Tiana blew up Dr. Syed's car, this was her first real kill.

She quickly rushed over and pressed the alarm button again to stop the ringing. Cee Cee pressed all of the elevator buttons, trying to get it moving again. She quickly took out the phone Vinny had given her, snapped a blurry picture of her victims, and started pulling the elevator doors open with her bare hands. Cee Cee gained strength she didn't know she had. The door opened enough for her to get her hands through and pull it wide enough for her to fit through.

The elevator was wedged between two floors when Cee Cee finally got the heavy door to open. She climbed over Linda's body and squeezed through the small opening between the elevator shaft and the ninth floor.

Cee Cee didn't realize she had blood all over the bottom of her boots, and her hoodie had blood splatter all over it from when she shot Pito. She scrambled up from the hallway floor and rushed to the door leading to the exit stairs. When she made it down to the sixth floor, Cee Cee heard distant screams coming from above.

Fuck! Already?

She knew the screams meant someone had found the bodies that fast. She started taking the stairs down two at a time with her heart threatening to bolt from her chest. Before she exited on the first floor, she shrugged out of her hoodie and tossed it into the first floor incinerator shoot. The oversized T-shirt she wore underneath was still enough to conceal her weapon.

Cee Cee swallowed hard and took a deep breath before she exited the building. Then she calmly walked out of the building, forgetting about the blood on the bottom of her boots. She didn't realize that, with every step, she was leaving bloody footprints.

As she made her way down the block, she could hear the wail of police sirens in the distance. Cee Cee sucked in a deep breath and hailed a cab. Nothing could beat the high she felt after committing the murders. Now she understood how her father felt when he did it, Cee Cee said to herself as she settled into the back of the cab. She felt like she could get used to this life, especially if the pay was right.

"Damn, you wasn't playing." Vinny smirked when Cee Cee showed him the cell phone picture of Pito and Linda slumped in the elevator. Marie sucked her teeth and stormed out of the room, garnering a sharp glare from Cee Cee.

"Well, here's a few dollars for your troubles," Vinny said, pushing a small stack across the table in Cee Cee's direction.

Cee Cee's eyebrows shot up into arches. "What the fuck is that?" she asked incredulously. "I can tell from just looking at it that that's not half of what you got for that job. Hell no!"

"I never said what you were going to get. We never discussed a price tag. You didn't want to sit by my side. You didn't want to be a part of my crew. So you get what I feel like giving you," Vinny said evilly. "You get the independent person pay," he taunted.

Cee Cee's head began spinning, and she felt heat rising from her feet into her chest. She cut Vinny a look that could've sliced the Hope Diamond in half. "Give me the full stacks you owe me," she said through her teeth.

"I don't owe you a motherfucking thing. You're a little girl with nothing, so take what I'm giving you and be fucking happy. Like you said, you don't need me. So now you go find a place to live and a man to fuck. This business is no place for little dumb girls who think they're tough," Vinny replied dismissively, twirling his toothpick between his gold teeth.

His words cracked the shell of Cee Cee's already fragile composure. "Nah. Give me what the fuck you owe me!" Cee Cee barked, her face flushed red as she rushed for Vinny. A wall of bodies quickly blocked her movement.

"Get the fuck out of here before you bite off more than you can chew," he snarled. "I don't have to give you shit! That's eighty-five hundred, half of what I got for the job. Take it or leave it. I don't give a flying fuck!"

Cee Cee made a move to her waistband but, before she could pull her gun, four of Vinny's security goons put hands on her.

Vinny started laughing. "What? You were going to shoot me with your little gun right here in my own house? Shit, that's not even your fucking gun to begin with. But I'll tell you what. I'm gonna let you keep it. Consider it a gift from me."

Cee Cee looked at him with daggers for eyes. If looks could kill, Vinny would have been dead right then.

"You think you're tough, don't you? If Louis taught you how to be smart then you better know who not to fuck with," Vinny said.

Cee Cee's jaw rocked feverishly and her chest heaved. The pressure from Vinny's goons clamping down on her arm became painful. "Get the fuck off me!" she yelled, wrestling her arms away. She snatched the stack of cash from the table and squinted at Vinny.

"You got this one for damn near free, but don't count me out of this game. You will pay me everything that you owe me. Everything," Cee Cee spat.

"Get the fuck out of here. You're just like that little weak bitch father of yours, always thinking people will be loyal and honest." Vinny waved her off.

Cee Cee started for him again, but she was quickly hoisted into the air.

"I had enough of your ass," Vinny said as she was dropped and fell to the floor. "Hold her down," he instructed one of his guys. While one of the guys held her arms above her head, he straddled her and put a pillow over her face. Cee Cee kicked and shook her head back and forth to try to catch her breath, but Vinny was holding the pillow over her face and had all his weight on it. When her body finally went completely limp, he removed the pillow to see Cee Cee's lifeless facial expression.

"And this is the way the fucking game is played," he said as he leaned in to speak into Cee Cee's ear as if she were still alive to hear what he was saying. "There's no honor among killers. Shit, I'd kill your mother for the right price," Vinny said, followed by a sinister laugh.

His security knew he was a crazy guy, but they never thought he'd go so far as to kill his own wife's daughter.

They all exchanged glances with each other but not a single one of them said a word.

"Get her out of here and make sure her mother doesn't see or find out about this," he said as he walked out of the room without bothering to look back.

Chapter 14

Drake dropped Tiana off at the apartment he got for her and he sped off. Instead of going inside, though, Tiana decided she needed to pay a certain someone a much-needed visit.

Tiana called a taxi and gave the driver the address to her destination. When she arrived, Tiana paid the driver and stepped out onto the cold, hard concrete. Tiana walked across a parking lot and then went onto a sidewalk. The familiar surroundings gave her ease and comfort. After being in her old house and seeing how run-down and abandoned it was, Tiana had an overwhelming need to feel connected to family.

Tiana used her fists to pound on the familiar door like the police were chasing her. She touched the gun she had stuffed in her waist to reassure herself that she had protection if she needed it. When no one came to the door, Tiana let out a long sigh and lifted the doorknocker. She pounded three times and waited.

"What?" someone barked from the other side of the door.

Tiana shook her head a little bit and smiled. It was true what they said about Puerto Ricans: old, young, fat, skinny, tall, or short, everybody was always damn angry. "*Madrina.* It's Tiana," she announced.

She could hear her godmother's hearty laugh as she clicked the fifty locks she had on her door. "*Ahijada!*" Mama Hilda said lovingly, pulling Tiana close for a tight squeeze against her ample bosom. "I missed you. Let me look at you," Mama Hilda sang, spinning Tiana around.

Tiana examined her godmother just as closely. She still had those beautiful round eyes and that creamy beige skin, but Mama Hilda was starting to look old. Tiana immediately noticed the half-moon laugh lines edging each side of Mama Hilda's mouth, the wrinkles branching from the corners of each of her eyes, and loose skin dangling under her neck like a turkey wattle. Mama Hilda still smelled like White Diamonds perfume just like Tiana remembered.

"I missed you too, *Madrina*. So much shit has happened since *Papi* died," Tiana lamented. "Everything is all messed up now," she said as she walked farther into the familiar house, making herself at home right away.

Mama Hilda was her father's right hand for all of the years he had been the top hitter in the streets. Mama Hilda held her own in the game and, legend had it, she was more ruthless than Griselda Blanco. Drake had told Tiana that Mama Hilda was the only one of her father's people who didn't go over to Lobo's new crew after her father's death. Mama Hilda stayed loyal to Marquez even after his death and she kept true to the Los Asesinos, but it hadn't been easy. There had been a few attempts on her life since Marquez's death. The other crews had also tried to shut her out, but she always managed to survive. People knew that Mama Hilda kept her AK-47 close at all times and she still had a few connections she could call in if there was an emergency.

"So what's up, goddaughter? Your stepmother locked you away and never told me where. I found out from Drake and when I went to go see you they said your doctor had put on a strict no-visitor's allowed policy. That bitch was always miserable and I always had a feeling she was a dirty snake. I never liked her. She was trash from the day I first laid eyes on her, and I told Marquez how I felt. He was so in love with that skank. The only good thing that ever came from that *puta* was how happy your dad seemed to be after he got with her. I never understood what he saw in her but it was nice to see him smiling and happy again. You made him happy and he loved you with all his heart, but his smile was never the same since your mother died. When Giselle came around, he was smiling and starting to act like his old self again. But look what she turned out to be. A goddamned sneaky bitch," Mama Hilda said with disgust. "I don't care what nobody says, she had something to do with your father's murder. And now she's lying up with that Angel guy. Rumor has it he's from Los Diablos. She is a fucking traitor as far as I am concerned. I don't trust either of them," Mama Hilda said with feeling.

"Yeah, that bitch tried to ruin me by having me put in there. But you know me, *Madrina*. I get knocked down, but I don't stay down. I'm out. I'm alive and I need to get myself together again. I'm back for good this time, *Madrina*. I want to try to get Los Asesinos going again. I want to keep my father's name alive," Tiana replied. "I got some people to take care of in order to do it, and I need to be smart about it. I need money to move and more equipment. I came to ask you for work. Anything."

"Oh, *ahijada,* I've been shut out since Marquez's murder. These fucks won't let me get in on anything. All I can get is little enforcer jobs. You know, a beating here, a threat there. Scaring and threatening people from time to time. Nothing big. I haven't had any big paydays. Shit, I miss getting blood on my hands, trust me," Mama Hilda admitted.

Tiana's shoulders slumped in disappointment. She thought at least Mama Hilda could help her.

"I tell you what," Mama Hilda said, shaking her head up and down like she was thinking hard. "Anything I hear about through the pipeline, I will let you know. Maybe if you start getting to their marks before they can, they will see their business drying up and come crawling. It will send them a message. I will keep my ear to the streets so we can fuck their heads up," Mama Hilda said, flashing her famous wide-toothed grin.

"Thanks, *Madrina*. I love you and I'll be waiting," Tiana replied.

"What? Leaving already?" Mama Hilda asked disappointedly.

"No, of course not. I can't leave until you cook me some food. I want to eat some of your famous *arroz con pollo*." Tiana smiled, pulling out a chair at the dining table. She was happy to still have someone who'd stayed loyal to her father.

Tiana was exhausted when she got back to the apartment that Drake had set up for her. She put her key in the door and rushed inside, yearning for a nice, warm shower and the bed.

Tiana looked around and was very happy with what she saw. Drake had hooked her up with a fully furnished one-bedroom apartment. The kitchen had black and silver marble countertops and white kitchen cabinets. It was stocked with stainless steel appliances and it even had a cute stainless steel teapot on the stove. The living room had a black suede sectional with black and cream pillows. The coffee table had a clear glass vase with silk red and white flowers. A fifty-four-inch flat screen was mounted on the wall.

"I love this place," Tiana whispered to herself, kicking off her sneakers and pulling her gun from her waist. She clicked on the light in the kitchen and went to the refrigerator to pour something to drink.

"Where were you?" Drake seemed to have appeared out of thin air.

"Oh, shit! What the fuck!" Tiana choked, sending the glass in her hand crashing to the floor.

"Calm down," Drake said, looking at her strangely. "Why you so nervous?"

"How the fuck you telling me to calm down when you lurking in the fucking apartment like a creep?" Tiana screamed at him. Her hands were still shaking fiercely. She didn't like the feeling of being snuck up on like that. "You lucky I had already put my gun down or your ass would be slumped right now," Tiana asserted.

Drake chortled and shook his head at her. "Yeah, a'ight, tough girl."

"Why the fuck you sneaking in here and shit?" Tiana gasped, still trying to catch her breath.

"Better question is, where the fuck you been and why the fuck you so nervous and jumpy?" Drake shot back, bending down to pick up the broken glass.

"Yo, Drake. For real. Right now is not the time to start that possessive shit." Tiana put her hand up. "I've been locked up for mad long with people telling me when to eat, think, sleep, shit. I don't need that from you. I have a lot of shit on my plate these days if you haven't noticed." Tiana knew it would only be a matter of time before Drake started acting overprotective. It never failed.

When Tiana and Drake were little kids they were inseparable best friends. They did everything together: played, fought, had sleepovers, went to school each day, fought off neighborhood bullies, cried, and laughed. They were more like close siblings than just friends. Although Drake was two years older than Tiana, he never treated her like she was younger than him. When they became teenagers, Drake began to get very overprotective of her. He would beat up any guy who approached her the wrong way or disrespected her. Everyone thought Tiana and Drake had something going on but the truth was Drake just wanted to make sure Tiana was safe.

Tiana loved having Drake as her best friend. She loved knowing that someone was always around to look out for her. Even after she moved to the "big house," as Drake called it, and they weren't able to see each other as often, Drake still stayed on top of her and made sure she was good. He was always there for her during times when she felt no one else cared and he was the best friend anyone could ever ask for.

What Tiana had failed to realize for so long was that Drake was secretly in love with her. He had loved her since they were teenagers. All the girls he ran around with were just pawns to help him pass the time. When Drake found out about the shootout at her house, he felt guilty that he wasn't around to help in any way. He saw how hard her father's death was on her. He did his best to cheer her up and get her to see that things were going to get better, but her depression just kept getting worse. He felt like a part of him was missing the entire year that she hadn't been around. Now that she was back he was going to make sure she was okay and that he wouldn't lose her again. He had already decided that he was going to make his move and finally confess his true feelings to her, and tonight was as good a night as ever.

"Me expecting you to check in with me and let me know where you are is not being possessive. It's called being worried. Your father still got enemies on the streets and your ass walking around with a fucking hit list and shit. You expect me not to worry? You came to me, remember?" Drake shot back. "Fuck me in the ass for being the person who cares most about you." He shook his head in disgust.

Tiana's face softened. She knew Drake was right. He was just trying to have her back at all times. Maybe she should have been letting him know her every move. "A'ight. You right, Drake. I'm sorry I didn't call you and let you know what was up," Tiana relented.

A slight smirk of satisfaction spread over Drake's face. "So where you been? Any place interesting?"

"I went to see Mama Hilda and finally got some home-cooked food. Satisfied?" Tiana reported in a playfully snide tone.

"Nah, not satisfied," Drake mumbled with a smile on his face. Then he rushed into her, grabbed her face roughly, and he covered his mouth over hers. He couldn't resist it anymore.

"What the—" Tiana started. Drake had caught her off guard, causing her to stumble backward clumsily.

"Tiana, I love you. I am in love with you and I don't want to keep it a secret anymore," he confessed. He then leaned back in and went in for another kiss.

"Mmmm," Tiana tried to protest, but Drake was too strong.

"Stop fighting me," he panted, holding on to her arms. The heat of his words danced over her lips.

"Stop," Tiana breathed out, exasperated. She didn't fight as hard as she would have if Drake were a stranger trying to take advantage of her, but she still didn't like feeling powerless.

"Nah, I've been waiting for you, for this. I missed you so much this past year. I love you," he whispered.

The words "I love you" softened Tiana at the edges. She could feel some of the tension she'd been feeling for days easing.

Drake pressed his body into hers until she was sandwiched between the kitchen wall and his muscular chest. Tiana tried to fight a little more, but Drake smelled and felt so good.

"Let me love you, Tiana. Let me," Drake panted into her ear. "Let me take care of you. Let me stop all of your pain and need for revenge."

Finally, Tiana relented. She relaxed her previously tense muscles and allowed her tongue to perform a sexy dance with Drake's. A tsunami of lust and love rushed Tiana all at once, threatening to drown her in the moment. Tiana always wanted to be touched in a gentle, loving way by someone who actually loved her. Drake moved his mouth from hers and trailed his tongue down her neck. A shockwave of electricity filled her loins. Tiana was feeling things she had never felt from any sexual experience she'd had.

"Drake, we can't," Tiana panted, the throbbing between her legs making them quiver. She couldn't understand why her body was betraying her when her mind was screaming, *no!* "We are crossing the line."

"Shhh. No, we're not," Drake mumbled just before he took in a mouthful of her left nipple. "I've been wanting this moment to happen for so long now."

Drake sucked Tiana's breasts gently, cupping each one like they were delicate pieces of crystal. Tiana let out a whimper when he licked around her areola softly and blew on them.

"Uhhh," Tiana panted as she felt parts of her body come alive with more electric pulses than she'd ever experienced. Drake unbuttoned her pants with the quickness and skill of a professional. Before Tiana could protest any further, he gently rubbed her clit with his moistened pointer finger until he was sure her love juices were flowing; then he stuck his middle finger into her dripping wet center.

"Shit," Tiana gasped. Drake added his pointer finger and pulled the two fingers in and out of her at the same time.

Suddenly Tiana's mind slipped to the past and her ears were invaded by the sound of Dr. Syed's voice: *"Hold her down so I can finger that tight hole and see what it tastes like."*

"No, wait," Tiana moaned, moving her head back and forth to fight off the intrusive memories.

"Look at me," Drake whispered. Tiana opened her eyes slightly and realized it was Drake. She watched as he licked her nectar from his fingers like it was the best thing he'd ever tasted.

"Oh, God," she breathed heavily. She couldn't keep the memories from crashing in on her.

"Hold her legs open!" Dr. Syed demanded. Two of his orderlies rushed over and held Tiana down. She was writhing and flailing, but she was no match for them. Then Dr. Syed's nurse came over with a wicked smile on her face.

"Lick that pussy. Turn her out," Dr. Syed commanded right before his nurse, Teema, planted her head between Tiana's legs.

"Anything for you," Teema groaned.

"Stop. Stop. No, wait," Tiana huffed, trying to push Drake away from her.

"No. I want to. I want to taste you," Drake panted just before he moved his head toward her pussy. He put his hot mouth over her clitoris and breathed on it. Tiana almost climbed the kitchen wall, her back arching against it until she was nearly floating. The fight between the present and the past had her mind swirling. She punched at Drake's shoulders but that just turned him on even more.

Drake licked, sucked, and blew air on her clit like a man possessed. Tiana moved her head left to right and used her hands to guide his head farther into her slick, moist box. Her legs were weak.

"I can't stand up," Tiana moaned.

"You taste so good," Drake whispered.

Then another voice filled Tiana's ears. *"She tastes so good. Mmmm, I love being a freak for you,"* Teema moaned.

Tiana had tears in her eyes now. "Please, I can't," she whimpered. He refused to give up. He got to his feet, looked Tiana in the eyes, and picked her up. "We can't," Tiana said, but she was so emotionally drained she had no fight left in her.

"Nah, we can. When shit is meant to be, it's just meant to be. This has always been meant to be," he said.

Drake carried her to the living room and gently placed her down on the couch. Tiana's head was swimming with a mixture of wanting, lust, and nightmarish memories. Drake was still her best friend. They were crossing the line. This might end their friendship if it didn't go well. He didn't know what she had been through. Tiana wasn't sure if she loved Drake the way he loved her. She knew there was an attraction between them, but she was afraid that doing this was going to ruin their friendship.

"This is a mistake. We can't. We shouldn't," Tiana huffed, her voice coming out throaty and hoarse. "You're my best friend."

"I have to have you. I can't take it anymore. I have always loved you, Tiana. Don't you understand that? I can't front no more," Drake replied with feeling. Tiana closed her eyes because his words were like sun on a patch of ice, melting her cold insides in that moment.

Drake kissed her again passionately. Then he stood up, pulled his pants off, and exposed his thick, throbbing tool. Tiana closed her eyes, spread her legs voluntarily and let go. She let go of all of the pain and hurt she'd been burdened with. She let go of her revenge plans for that moment. She let go of her hard girl exterior. But, more importantly, as Drake gently slid himself deep into her dripping wet center, Tiana let go of her inhibitions and for the moment she forgot about all of the abuse she'd suffered in the past year.

"Yes. Yes," she murmured as Drake moved inside of her with care like someone who loved her.

"I love you, Tee," Drake murmured into the soft skin between her neck and shoulder. Tiana didn't answer him; instead, she began moving her hips in conjunction with his until their bodies made a sweet rhythm that danced through her soul. Even if the feeling was temporary for her, Tiana enjoyed every minute of it.

The next morning, when Tiana awoke, Drake was gone. She sat up slowly in the bed and looked around for him. She squinted when she noticed a piece of paper on the pillow Drake had slept on. Tiana picked it up slowly. A pang of fear and rejection coiled through her stomach. She read it.

René Rodriguez: Caliente downtown (hangs out at the club, usually stays in hotel on Rashelle Drive after, whole penthouse floor)
Dana Shaw: Maplewood Village apartments. Apt #32
Teema Chambers: still can't find

Tiana smiled and held the paper up against her chest. "Fucking Drake. You're the fucking man. You never fail to come through for me," she said aloud with a big, cheesy grin on her face. Drake had kept his promise of helping her find the people on her list. She loved Drake and she was still worried about how what happened between them last night was going to affect their relationship.

Chapter 15

S. Gates sat with his hands clasped together in front of him, listening to the sound of the recording. All of the men in the room held their breath, waiting for his reaction. S. Gates slowly lifted his head until his face was noticeable. A raised vein at his temple pulsed so fiercely against his caramel skin it could be seen from distance.

"So, tell me again. This was retrieved from the laptop of an employee of the hospital my brother worked at?" Gates asked evenly.

"Yes, boss," Blaine answered. He had been the one to get the recording from S. Gates's paid insider at Flint PD.

"Miss Caldoron." He repeated that last name he'd heard on the recording.

"Yes, boss. That's the name this guy said to someone who was in the apartment with him before he was killed. Apparently this was someone he was familiar with. The guys are going over everything now to set up a time line and to see if they think there is a link between what happened to your brother and son and what happened to this guy. I mean, since your brother worked with this guy and all," Blaine answered.

"You just showed me building security camera footage of a woman going into the building wearing exactly what the woman in my brother's video was wearing, and you telling me they haven't made the connection yet?" S. Gates replied, sitting up stiffly in his chair.

"From what they said, they're pretty sure that there is a connection, but they want to be—" Blaine started.

"Fuck what they said!" Gates shouted, slamming his palms down on the long table. All eyes were on him, but none dared to look him directly in his eyes.

"They think I am a legitimate businessman, too! They have no fucking idea I'm probably being hit by somebody vying for my spot in the drug game! So I don't give a fuck what they said and what they think!" he roared. Then he closed his eyes for a few seconds, adjusted his Hermès tie, and cleared his throat. He hated losing his cool. He had always believed that a man who couldn't keep his composure and keep his emotions in check was weak.

"I am putting a hundred thousand on the head of whoever is responsible for my son's murder. If this Miss Caldoron person is connected to René and the Diablos, I want every single one of their men dead. I don't care if I have to go out there on my own and find this bitch, whoever she is. I want her brought to me alive so I can look into her eyes. I want to see her suffer before she dies. Let all of my street distributors know that I am looking for this girl. I want her brought to me alive, and I want all the information you can get on her. Find out who she is, who she loves, what she loves, and destroy it all," S. Gates commanded. The fact that he went from zero to one hundred and then back to zero scared all of his men, and the fear in the room was almost tangible.

S. Gates stood up and stormed out of the conference room. All of his men clamored out behind him. They had a message to send to the streets and a job to do.

The Meringue music reverberated off the walls of Club Caliente and pulsed through Tiana's body. Even though she was Puerto Rican, she'd always hated that type of music and now was no different. She'd grin and bear it for tonight, though, because she was here with a purpose. She had a mission she needed to complete.

Sitting alone at the bar, Tiana looked out into the club as the partygoers swayed their bodies and moved their hips and feet so fast to the music that a few of them looked like they were running in place. Tiana gave off the vibe that she belonged there, which was all part of her plan.

Tiana was a far cry from when she wore her black hoodie, oversized T-shirt, black pants, and sneakers. Tonight, she had let her hair loose and it fell in dark coils down her back. She dressed in a shocking red form-fitting jersey dress that accentuated her heart-shaped booty and her thick thighs. She matched the jersey dress with a pair of wedge heels that made her look model tall, and she had gone to the mall and gotten her makeup done at the MAC counter. She knew she was looking good because the second she walked into the place she felt all eyes on her. She made her way to the bar and the bartender quickly asked her what she wanted to drink. She smiled coyly at the bartender and asked for a coconut Cîroc and pineapple juice on the rocks.

Tiana nursed her drink as she took in the sights of the club, namely her mark, René Rodriguez, who was, of course, surrounded by throngs of women and a phalanx of his top men and security.

René Rodriguez was the head of the Diablos, the Dominican faction of hit men who worked for some of the most dangerous drug cartels in the United States. Tiana's father had been the head of Los Asesinos, the Puerto Rican faction of hit men who mostly worked for the rival cartels. Everyone knew Dominicans hated Puerto Ricans and vice versa, so when Tiana had heard René's name come up as a possible suspect in her father's murder, it was all she needed to add him to her list.

She watched René from afar for a while, but she knew she couldn't get all of the information she needed from that far away. After a little while at the bar, Tiana decided it was time for her to try to get a little closer. She wanted to hear René's voice, watch his movements, and look into his eyes.

Tiana jumped down from the barstool she had been holding down and suddenly she felt a tight grasp on the upper part of her arm. Her body stiffened and she clutched her purse, where she had one of her father's knives sandwiched between two maxi pads: the only way she could sneak it into the club. Tiana turned to the person touching her.

"I was just going to ask if I could buy you a drink," the person said, quickly letting her go when he saw the angry scowl on her face.

"You should never approach a woman and grab up on her like that," Tiana spat, shooting daggers at him with her eyes. "A simple, 'Can I buy you a drink?' without you putting your hands on me might've gotten you somewhere," she hissed.

Although Tiana's nostrils were flaring and her left hand curled into a fist on its own, she couldn't help but notice how fine the stranger was. His skin was smooth like newly melted caramel, his deep-set eyes were adorned by the thickest, longest lashes Tiana had ever seen on a man, and the dark, tight curls that hugged his head were perfectly cut and lined up. He was also dressed nicely in an expensive French-cuff button-up shirt, Ferragamo belt, and a sleek pair of black slacks.

"I apologize about that. I really didn't mean to startle you," the gorgeous stranger said as he looked deep into her eyes. "I usually don't approach women in clubs. But you're beautiful. I couldn't risk you getting away."

A flash of shame and embarrassment lit Tiana's cheeks aflame. She shifted her weight from one foot to the other and broke eye contact with the man. Hearing someone call her beautiful immediately sent her brain into defensive mode. The last time she'd heard she was beautiful had been from Dr. Syed right before he forced himself on her for the first time.

"Thanks. But, I don't take drinks from strangers," she said flatly before rushing away from the man. As much as Tiana would have loved to sit and chat with him, now was not the time for her to make small talk. She had to stick to her plans and do what she came here to do.

Tiana could feel the heat of his gaze on her as she made her way to an area of the lounge that was closer to the VIP section. Tiana took a seat where she could hear René partying raucously. Women surrounded him as he tossed handfuls of one hundred dollar bills in the air, laughing as the women scrambled around on the floor like hungry dogs trying to grab handfuls of the money.

"You. I want you," René slurred, pointing to a tall, slim blonde with large, fake breasts. Tiana watched as the girl rushed over and put her balloon-looking breasts in René's face and then dumped a small mound of cocaine on them. He leaned in and snorted the thin white line. René threw his head back and laughed.

"My kind of woman!" he yelled as he buried his face in her chest. Loud laughter followed.

Tiana watched René snort at least six lines of cocaine and chase them down with shot after shot of Patrón. By the time the VIP section was almost cleared out René could hardly stand. He and the blonde were fondling and licking each other as his crew tried to urge him to leave.

"I'm the fucking boss. I say when it's time," René slurred in Spanish. Tiana knew that if it weren't for his security being so deep she could've taken René out right there in the club.

Tiana looked at her cell phone clock. It was already four o'clock in the morning. She remembered Drake's note saying that René usually opted to stay in the city at the Hampton Inn after wild nights of partying. Tiana left Club Caliente and headed to the hotel. It would take some skill to get past all of the security and get close to René, but she was confident in her abilities.

"*Buenas noches,*" Tiana said, smiling sweetly at the concierge behind the desk.

The man nodded at her and smiled politely. "Good evening, ma'am," he responded.

"Señor René sent me. He's had a wild night and wants me to prepare his bath and things before he gets here," Tiana said, sounding as official as she could. The man behind the desk made a face that read a mixture of confusion and suspicion.

"I know it seems strange, but you know him . . . very wild," Tiana said, using her hands to depict a sexual act. "He told me you might be hesitant, you know, for his protection, so he also told me to give you this and for you not to mention it to his men. They don't really know some of the things he is into," Tiana said, sliding five one-hundred-dollar bills across the counter in his direction. The money from her father's bag was coming in handy.

"Ah, yes, I certainly understand." The man smiled, quickly placing his hand on top of the cash and sliding it off the counter. "You know how to go from here, correct?" he asked as he handed her the access card to his room.

"Of course," Tiana sang, winking at the man as she snatched the card and headed for the elevators.

"Shit, I hope Drake was right about it being the entire penthouse floor," she mumbled to herself.

Almost an hour later, Tiana heard when René and his companion for the night entered the suite. A rush of excitement and nervousness flooded Tiana's body, causing her skin to feel tingly and sensitive. "Catching someone off guard is not weak; it's smart," her father had taught her when he was teaching her the ropes.

Now, Tiana listened to the sounds of smacking and sucking, and she pictured René and the blonde from the club tongue-kissing and fondling each other.

"Let me go freshen up," Tiana heard the blonde call out in Spanish.

"Hurry up!" she heard René reply.

Tiana's heart raced as she heard the blonde step into the bathroom and lock the door. Tiana peeked out from a small opening in the pulled shower curtain and she watched the blonde undress. She watched as the girl took her bra off and grabbed her breasts as if she needed to readjust her nasty implants. As Tiana watched the blonde finish undressing, something caught her eye.

Oh, shit! Tiana cupped her hands over her mouth and watched the blonde grab on to his dick, stand over the toilet, and take a piss.

Tiana shook her head. *Holy shit! It's a shemale! Damn, he look better than some women! René the so-called boss about to take it in the ass?*

As the shemale finished, Tiana gripped her father's hunting knife until her knuckles paled. She knew the transgender would probably be coming to take a shower next and would find her standing behind the shower curtain. Tiana was ready.

The blonde went into his purse and retrieved a small glassine envelope of cocaine, dumped a tiny mound onto the back of his hand, held it up against his nostril, and inhaled deeply.

"Ah! I'm going to need this to fuck this old, nasty motherfucker," the shemale whispered. "And he ain't fucking me in my ass this time. Ugly-ass motherfucker always walking around thinking he's God's gift. Lucky he got some coin."

"Ay! C'mon!"

Tiana and the shemale both jumped when René banged on the bathroom door and started yelling for the blonde to hurry up.

"I'm coming, baby!" the shemale called out coquettishly. "Shut the fuck up and wait," the shemale grumbled quietly, grabbing the shower curtain and yanking it back. The blonde's eyes widened and his mouth dropped open in utter surprise when he saw someone standing in the tub with a knife in her hand. He was so shocked, the scream was stuck somewhere between his lungs and his throat and wouldn't come out.

"Shhhh," Tiana warned, putting the point of her knife up against the shemale's throat.

The shemale closed his eyes and swallowed hard. Tears immediately drained from the corners of his eyes. "Please, I don't even know him. He's just a john to me," he whispered. "I have nothing to do with his business. I'm not the one you want. I just get paid to be here."

"Get on your knees," Tiana whispered back harshly, pushing the knife into the blonde's skin just enough to draw a drop of blood. He silently did as he was told. Tiana reached over and turned the shower on so that René wouldn't hear anything.

"How many men came up here with him?" Tiana whispered gruffly in the shemale's ear. The blonde shrugged his shoulders. Tiana got behind him and clutched on to a handful of his hair.

"Oh, shit," Tiana huffed, as the blond wig came off into her hand and scared her. "Fuck," she panted, tossing the wig into the sink next to her. Tiana quickly recovered and put the blade of the hunting knife to the shemale's throat.

"I'll ask you again: how many men are out there?" Tiana whispered through clenched teeth, holding the knife perilously close to the shemale's throat.

"They're in the adjoining room. He . . . he wanted to be alone with me," he sobbed. "Nobody knows my . . . my secret, so he doesn't allow them in the suite with us. They are all fucked up and probably asleep or fucking some of the whores he keeps around. He was supposed to be here for the night. They said they did a sweep before we came up here," the shemale relayed. "Please, just let me go. I'm just here to make some money," he cried.

"I'm sorry, boo, but I can't let you go," Tiana said as she pushed the blade farther into his neck. Tiana pulled and slid the knife blade across his throat with so much force she could hear the skin ripping apart. The shemale's body folded to the floor.

"I just couldn't risk you running off and snitching," Tiana spoke more to herself than to the now dead transgender on the floor. She stepped back and watched as the dark burgundy blood ran from the deep cut in the shemale's throat and quickly seeped onto the floor. Tiana yanked a towel down from the rack and pushed it under the door. She couldn't afford for the blood to leak under the door and alert René that something was amiss.

"Your turn now, faggot nigga," Tiana grumbled, taking the blond wig and pulling it down onto her head. When she stepped out of the bathroom into the suite, the room was pitch black. Tiana hesitated a few seconds, letting her eyes adjust to the darkness. In the darkness she could hear loud snoring coming from the bed. Tiana craned her neck and squinted until she could see René's buck-naked silhouette sprawled out on the bed. Tiana carefully inched to the bedside, picked up René's tie, a pair of handcuffs, and a black whip that was lying on the floor.

Guess you was about to get your S and M freaky shit on, huh, nasty nigga? Tiana chortled silently in her head.

Slowly and quietly Tiana moved with the sneakiness of a sly fox. When she finished cuffing René to the bed, she carefully climbed on, took his tie, and tied it around his mouth. René finally came alive from his deep tequila- and cocaine-induced slumber.

"Mmm. Mmmm," he moaned, trying in vain to fight the unknown force overtaking him.

"Shhh, or I cut your dick off and shove it down your throat," Tiana whispered, an evil grimace tugging at the corners of her mouth. Even in the darkness she could see hints of terror on his face.

René flailed a little bit more, moaning and grunting at Tiana.

"You must be making threats behind that gag, huh? Well, your threats don't mean shit to me. Yes, I know who you are," Tiana growled, clicking on the lamp next to the bed. "Seems like I keep catching all of you motherfuckers in bed slipping," Tiana said, rubbing the tip of her knife close to René's left eye. "Funny how all of you perverts keep getting caught with your dicks out." she chortled. "You're probably wondering who I am and why I'm here," she said, not expecting an answer.

René moved his head up and down.

"You should know who your enemies are, René. I thought you were a smart man," Tiana taunted. "This is for Los Asesinos," she said as she moved her knife toward his heart. René felt the tip of the knife penetrate the skin and his eyes went wide. He began moving wildly, but to no avail. Tiana smiled as she looked into René's eyes. Seeing the fear dancing behind his drunken eyes fueled her wrath even more.

"So you've figured it out?" She laughed.

René began trying to speak through the material of the tie.

"You want to tell me something?" Tiana said in an eerie little girl voice. She sounded like a deranged character from a scary movie. She cut away the material of the tie. Although it was risky, something inside of Tiana wanted to hear René's last words before she exacted her revenge.

René went to open his mouth but Tiana placed the sharp tip of the knife at his lips.

"Scream and I'll cut your fucking tongue out," she warned. "Now, tell me, what is it you have to tell me? Your dying declaration," she hissed.

"I . . . I have a deal with Los Asesinos. Why have they sent you?" René panted, sweating dripping down the sides of his face.

"A deal? Yeah, right, you fucking liar," Tiana replied, her eyebrows furrowed. "What deal are you talking about?"

"Yes. Yes. The new deal. The one that changed your crew from Los Asesinos to Asesinos Sicopata." René rushed his words out.

Tiana's eyebrows dipped even lower on her face. "What the fuck are you talking about?"

"When we took out the Los Asesinos leader so that Lobo could take over and get more money for hits, we agreed to rotate high-priced hits between our crews. When we made the arrangement, we agreed to no more wars. We . . . we are all family now so I don't understand this attack," René huffed out. He was speaking like he hadn't been high out of his mind a few minutes earlier. Tiana had obviously blown his high, but now he was blowing hers.

Tiana squinted her eyes as her heartbeat sped up from the information she was hearing. "Lobo?" Tiana started.

"Yes, yes. See, Lobo set up the Los Asesinos old boss, Marquez. Lobo had started sleeping with Marquez's woman and together he and the bitch made a plan to take

Marquez out. Lobo and some of the other Los Asesinos guys were fed up with the chump change Marquez was paying for hits and they didn't like that he had so many moral rules about kids and women, so we made the arrangement. Lobo gave us Marquez's home address, Marquez's wife gave the signal that Marquez was home and, with the blessing of the top dealers in the city, we went to his home and took him out," René rattled off, the information flowing from his mouth like a river. Tiana couldn't believe the way such an allegedly dangerous head hit man was spilling his guts out of fear. Wasn't there some code they should follow?

Tiana felt like the room was spinning around her and she could no longer control her breathing. The entire place had taken on a red hue like someone had pulled a red veil over her eyes.

"Lobo and my stepmother set my father up?" Tiana asked through clenched teeth. She wasn't expecting an answer, but repeating what she had just heard made it seem more plausible to her.

"Your father? Marquez was your father?" René replied, shock registering on his face and in his voice. "Fuck," he gasped. Then he went to scream but before any sound escaped his mouth Tiana drove her knife straight down into it. Tiana pressed the end of the knife until the blade had gone all the way into the back of René's throat. His body bucked and ghastly wheezing sounds escaped his mouth. Tiana closed her eyes and pressed on the knife handle until René's body went still. Tiana hadn't even realized how hard she was crying.

She pulled the knife out and looked at the blood dripping from the end of it. She rubbed her finger over the blade until blood covered her pointer finger. Then she walked over to the mirror over the dresser and used her blood-soaked finger to write a message.

LOS ASESINOS STILL LIVES.

Tiana knew the message would be sent to the Diablos, which would cause a chain reaction that she hoped hit Lobo directly. They didn't know it yet, but Lobo and Giselle had just made their way up to number one on her hit list.

Chapter 16

The sound of the gunshots snatched Lobo and Giselle out of their sleep.

"Oh my God!" Giselle gasped, leaping out of the bed like someone had shocked her with a thousand bolts of electricity. Lobo rolled off of the bed onto the floor with such a hard thud the wind was knocked out of him.

"Fuck," he gasped when three more gunshots resounded from somewhere in the apartment. Searching around in the darkness, Lobo located and grabbed the MP-5 he kept at his bedside at all times. "Go," he growled at Giselle. They had talked about this exact scenario more than once.

"I don't want to leave—" she cried.

"Go!" Lobo growled, cutting her off. She would just make things worse. Lobo got low and waited for the shooters to bust into this bedroom. Giselle made a mad dash for their walk-in closet, where she cowered behind shoeboxes and racks of clothes.

Just like Lobo suspected, his bedroom door came crashing in a few minutes later.

"Ah! Motherfuckers!" Lobo screamed, getting to his feet and spraying bullets at the door. "You come into my fucking house? Huh! You think I'm a fucking pussy! Huh!" he screamed.

After a few seconds and no sign of anybody, Lobo stopped shooting. The eerie silence caused the hairs on his neck to stand up. He slowly inched toward the door, his gun out in front of him. Moving forward like a military officer on a mission, Lobo whipped his head around but didn't see or hear anyone.

"Don't hide, *putas*. I'm right fucking here!" Lobo screamed, raising his gun menacingly. "I'm right fuckin'—"

Suddenly a sharp pain crashed into Lobo's shoulder like he'd been hit with a sledgehammer. His words tumbled back down his throat like hard marbles and his gun flew from his hands.

"Agh!" Lobo screamed as his body lurched forward and crumpled to the floor. Another searing pain hit him, this time in his left butt cheek.

"Urgh!" Lobo growled from the pain, spit popping from his lips and veins cording against the skin in his neck and face. Breathing heavily and barely able to control his own movements, Lobo flipped onto his back and right away came eye to eye with the source of his pain.

"Don't shoot me again, please. What do you want?" Lobo begged with his hands up defensively in front of him. "I have money in the safe. I have drugs. What do you want?" he cried, shaking all over.

Out of the corner of his eye he could see the doors to his bedroom terrace swinging open. He had been concentrating so hard on his bedroom door he'd forgotten about the other doors.

"Get him up," Andres commanded. Four men with guns rushed over and hoisted Lobo up into his own leather recliner. Lobo could feel his legs going numb, and the pain in his ass throbbed with every rapid pound of his heart. Lobo recognized the man who'd shot him.

"What the fuck are you doing, Andres? Where is René? What is this about?" Lobo hollered, his body rocking from the pain.

"So you're going to play stupid now?" Andres gritted, his eyes flashing with fire. He pointed his gun to Lobo's head.

"What the fuck are you talking about? I thought this was some fucking robbery and then I see you. Where the fuck is René?" Lobo barked, his voice crackling with agony.

"You sent someone to kill my boss and now you want to act like you don't know shit?" Andres growled, lifting his gun and bringing it down on Lobo's head. Andres was the Diablos second-in-command and René's right hand. Andres was much more ruthless than his boss and right now he was out for blood.

"Agh! Wait! What?" Lobo squawked, putting his hands up in defense. "I . . . I don't know what the fuck you're talking about. René is dead? No fucking way! I didn't order that hit, I swear," Lobo cried pleadingly. Lobo panted out a few breaths to try to stave off the pain rocking his body. He couldn't believe that the head of the Diablos was dead, but he could understand now why Andres had come ready to avenge his boss's death.

Andres stood back, rubbing his chin as he watched Lobo writhe in pain. Something in Lobo's eyes told Andres that maybe the sniveling man in front of him could be telling the truth. "I'm going to give you a chance to tell me what you know before I use this gun to blow your head off," Andres grumbled, waving his gun in Lobo's face.

"Listen, I . . . I wouldn't step on our peace agreement, I swear. Everything was going good. We are all making money with no problems. I didn't do it," Lobo panted. "Tell me what happened to René. There must be some reason you thought it was me. But, I swear, it wasn't."

Andres squinted and pursed his lips. "Someone tied him up, buck-naked, and drove a knife down his fucking throat like he was an animal to slaughter," Andres reported, his voice cracking with emotion. "On the mirror they wrote this in his fucking blood," Andres said, putting his cell phone screen in front of Lobo's face.

Lobo's eyes hooded over and he began breathing heavily as he examined the cell phone picture of the words written in blood.

LOS ASESINOS STILL LIVES.

"So, you're telling me that you had nothing to do with this?" Andres said through gritted teeth. "If you didn't then you have a snake in your crew and you're getting set up."

"There could only be one person who would do this, and I will save the Diablos the trouble and handle her myself," Lobo said, moving to stand up; but he was immediately forced back down into the chair from the pain of his gunshot wounds.

"I want whoever is responsible to suffer and I want proof. If you don't handle it and prove to me that it was someone else who murdered him, I will come back to you and finish what I started here. Don't fuck with me or I swear I will be back. The Diablos will fucking murder all of your people and all of their families. We are already at war. There is no turning back now," Andres said with assurance, getting close to Lobo's face.

"Now, you better think up a story for the police. Can't get treatment for gunshots without a story. Maybe you should say your bitch did it," Andres said snidely as he waved his goons toward the door.

Lobo slid out of the recliner and fell to the floor. He couldn't feel his legs. Grunting and struggling, Lobo used his arms to drag himself toward the bed.

"I am going to get this bitch and she is going to pay for this shit," Lobo grunted, out of breath.

Giselle was still cowering in the closet, wondering what the hell had just happened.

***

Tiana jumped out of her sleep covered in sweat. She looked around the room realizing she was at her apartment and not locked in a padded room. "Damn, that dream was real," she panted, laying the palm of her right hand on her rapidly rising chest.

As usual, the other side of the bed was empty. Drake had snuck out again while she slept. Drake had been staying with her on and off, but he was always leaving at all hours of the night. So far things were still cool between them and there hadn't been any awkwardness.

"This nigga be playing games," Tiana grumbled. She reached over to the nightstand and picked up the phone Drake had given her. There were a bunch of missed calls. Tiana crinkled her face in confusion.

"Only a few people have this number. What the fuck is going on?" she huffed, placing the phone to her ear to retrieve the voice mails. Tiana listened to the third message and felt like someone had reached into her chest and squeezed her heart until it stopped beating. The pleading voice filtering through the phone spurned her into action.

Tiana sprang to her feet like she had been splashed with ice-cold water. She whirled around in circles trying to find clothes to put on.

"Shit!" she huffed, almost falling over as she put on her jeans. Tiana grabbed both of her guns, holstered them, and put them on her waist. She grabbed two of her father's knives and threw them into a small black knapsack.

"I'm coming. I'm coming," she said aloud. Tiana raced out of the apartment building without doing the usual check of her surroundings. She didn't even notice that she was being watched.

Tiana made it to Mama Hilda's apartment in less than twenty minutes. She dug for the key Mama Hilda had given her on her last visit, but when Tiana went to put the key in the door, she realized she didn't need it. The door creaked open.

"Nah," Tiana whispered, her heart threatening to come up out of her throat. There was no way Mama Hilda would've left her door unlocked. She was probably more paranoid and more careful than Tiana's father on his best day. Tiana quickly retrieved her Glock from her holster before she stepped fully inside.

"*Madrina?*" Tiana called out apprehensively. "*Madrina,* you here? I got your messages. I'm sorry it took me so long to come."

There was no answer, but Tiana could hear a television playing loudly somewhere to her left. Tiana crept farther inside the apartment, but she didn't see anyone. Tiana moved slowly over to the spot in the living room where Mama Hilda kept her AK. Tiana peeked behind the couch and noticed the AK was gone. Suddenly, Tiana's body felt cold, like she was standing barefoot on a block of ice. A sharp pain started at the base of her skull and her head began pounding.

"*Madrina?*" Tiana yelled out, this time louder and more frantically than before. Tiana started moving around the apartment faster with her gun extended in front of her. When she got to Mama Hilda's bedroom Tiana slowly pushed the door open. The television was blasting the Spanish news channel.

"*Madrina!*" Tiana called out loudly. Once she stepped all the way into the room her legs went weak and she almost crumpled to the floor.

"No! *Madrina!* No!" Tiana squealed as she took in the sight of Mama Hilda's decapitated head sitting atop the television stand.

"Argh!" Tiana leaned over and threw up on the floor and, as she did, she quickly sprang to her feet and stumbled backward to get away from Mama Hilda's amputated arms.

"Oh, God!" Tiana cried out, whirling around. Behind her was Mama Hilda's naked torso, missing the legs and breasts. "No!" Tiana screamed, her body quaking all over. As she went to back out of the door, Tiana noticed the message on the wall behind Mama Hilda's bed written in blood.

I KNOW WHAT YOU DID. YOU CAN'T GET AWAY WITH IT. BE WARNED.

Tiana involuntarily bent over at the waist and threw up again. It wasn't the smell of blood that had made her sick; she was used to that. It wasn't even the brutality of the crime; she was used to that too. Tiana felt sick to her stomach to think that her godmother had been brutally tortured like that. She knew shit was only gonna get harder from here on out. The fact that they came after her godmother meant that they must have figured out that she was responsible for Rene's murder.

Tiana felt like her heart had been ripped out of her chest. She knew she had to get out of there and get herself together. There was no way she was going to let them get away with this.

Chapter 17

Drake rushed into Tiana's place like he was sprinting to save her life. As soon as Tiana saw his face, she rushed into him and broke down until her knees went weak.

"Whoa, whoa, Tee," Drake said as he held her in a tight embrace. Tiana melted against him, sobbing. "Shhh. Tell me what happened," Drake comforted her, rubbing Tiana's head. He hadn't gotten the street news about Mama Hilda's death yet.

"They fucking cut her up like a pig, Drake! They cut her head off and her . . . her arms!" Tiana cried, her body racked with sobs.

"What? Who?" Drake asked, moving Tiana from his chest so he could look into her eyes. "Who?" Drake shook her shoulders slightly.

"Mama Hilda! Agh!" Tiana screamed, becoming weak in the knees again. "I'm going to fucking kill all of them, Drake! I'm going to cut their fucking insides out! She was the only connection to my father I had left!"

"What the fuck? Who would want to kill her now? I mean, with the truce between the Diablos and the Asesinos Sicopata there was no reason to go after her," Drake said, flustered with disbelief.

"They wanted to send a message!" Tiana said, sniffling back snot and tears.

"But why? Everybody knows Mama Hilda is still con- nected to all of the cartel assassins in some way or another. She kept her loyalty to Marquez, but they already agreed to leave her alone after the last time they tried to take her out. They lost about ten of their men trying to take her out so they sent out the message that no one was to fuck with her," Drake said as she held on to Tiana.

"It was a message for me, Drake," Tiana said, pulling away from him. "I'm telling you, it was a message for me. Somebody knew I would be crushed by this," Tiana told him, looking at him pitifully.

"Nah. That doesn't make any sense. People don't even know you're back out here," Drake said. "There's gotta be some other shit going on."

"I'm telling you, they did this to her to fuck with me. They all know Mama Hilda was my heart. They wrote a message to me in her blood, Drake," Tiana said. Her voice quivered and tears started falling from her eyes again. "Shit keeps happening to me. It's like karma."

"But why?" Drake asked. "Do you think it has something to do with your list?"

"It was the Diablos," Tiana rasped, almost whispering. "It was the fucking Diablos," she said again through clenched teeth.

"Nah. They ain't got no time for shit like this, Tiana. I'ma keep my ear to the street and find out what happened, but for right now you ain't going nowhere without me," Drake said, pulling her back into his chest and holding her tight.

Tiana remained quiet. She didn't confess what she'd done to René Rodriguez but, in her heart, she felt that Mama Hilda's brutal murder was payback for that. Tiana was too scared to tell Drake exactly why she knew that the Diablos might be after her. Now, she would have to take care of them before she finished taking care of the people on her list.

***

Tiana handed the homeless-looking man a brown paper bag with the cash inside just like he'd instructed. He smelled like a garbage dump, but from what Tiana had heard, the man was paid. There were no words exchanged between Tiana and him, which was fine with her. She snatched the small drawstring bag, slung it over her shoulder, and walked away as briskly and quietly as she came.

Back at her apartment she examined the sticks of explosives like they were bars of gold. "Y'all didn't know who y'all fucking with," Tiana mumbled as she bound the sticks into bundles of four. She needed to get her explosives all set and ready. She knew how to make small bombs like the one she had made for Dr. Syed's car, but this was on a whole other level. She needed to get some legit ones that would get the big job done.

"Mama Hilda, I will never forget you. You will live with me for life. They won't get away with what they did to you," Tiana said out loud.

The next day, Tiana watched from a distance as Mama Hilda was given the grand funeral she deserved. Some of the biggest drug kingpins were in attendance and so were Drake, Lobo, Giselle, the Asesinos Sicopata, and the Diablos. Tiana counted six Diablos, including Andres, their new leader who'd taken the reins after René's murder.

Drake had insisted on attending the funeral in Tiana's place. He refused to let Tiana risk attending the big elaborate service, fearful that whoever killed Mama Hilda might be coming around today. If they really had killed Mama Hilda to get to Tiana, they were sure to be waiting for her to show up. He didn't want to risk putting her in harm's way. He still wasn't 100 percent convinced that Mama Hilda's murder had anything to do with Tiana but, still, he tried to keep Tiana close in the days after the funeral, leaving her only for short periods at a time so he could conduct his business. Tiana took advantage of every one of those times she was alone to get her next moves clearly planned out.

Now, she was bent down behind two huge, ancient-looking slate gray mausoleums; and she dialed Drake's cell number. Tiana watched from her hiding spot as Drake dug into his suit jacket and walked away from the crowd of funeral-goers to answer.

"Drake, it's me. I need you to leave right now. I need you," Tiana whispered.

"Tee, where are you? What's going on?" Drake huffed into the phone, his head moving like it was on a swivel.

"Just leave now. Get the fuck out of there, Drake," Tiana whispered harshly. "Leave now for your own good." From her hiding spot, she watched Drake rush toward his car. Tiana was counting in her head. Everything was a numbers game. Everything was about time. Her father had taught her that lesson over and over again.

Drake was six cars away from the Diablos vehicles. Not enough distance to be sure that he would be safe. "C'mon, Drake. Leave already," Tiana mumbled under her breath. Drake was seemingly taking forever to get out of there.

"Finally." She sighed and her shoulders fell with relief when Drake drove away from the long line of cars. She would explain her frantic phone call to him later.

"Daddy and Mama Hilda, they are about to get what they deserve for what they did to y'all. May they all rot in hell," Tiana said out loud as if her father and Mama Hilda were standing in front of her.

Tiana ducked lower when she noticed the burial service breaking up. Tiana's heart rate sped up with excitement as she watched the attendees shuffle toward their cars. Tiana got low to the ground and moved downhill in the cemetery until she was sure she was a safe distance away.

She could still see the marks' cars in the distance. Tiana recognized Andres and three of the Diablos top men as they climbed into the silver Suburban. She was grateful that Mama Hilda had given her a file full of pictures and information on Los Diablos and the new members that had joined Lobo's Asesinos Sicopata crew before she passed. She wanted to make sure her goddaughter was well informed and up to date with everything that had been going on during the year that she had been at Rollins.

The driver let his bosses into the vehicle and then rushed to the front and climbed inside. The black Escalade in front of them also carried Diablos members.

"Shit!" Tiana cursed when she saw Lobo walk over and knock on the window of the silver Suburban. "You better get the fuck away," Tiana whispered. Although Lobo was on her list, Tiana wanted to see him in person, later.

Lobo walked away and started toward his vehicle, which was five cars away. Before Lobo fully reached his vehicle, the driver of the silver Suburban keyed the ignition.

Boom! Boom! The blast sent Tiana reeling backward, and a cloud of dust that resembled a huge tornado rose into the sky.

Screams erupted everywhere. The force of the blast sent Lobo face first into the dirt and several other people were knocked down by the blast. Cemetery headstones were torn from the ground and went flying into the air. The silver Suburban and the black Escalade were both completely engulfed in flames. The entire place erupted into massive chaos with people running and screaming.

Tiana got off her back and raced down the hill on the far side of the cemetery. Her ears were ringing and her head pounded from the sound of the blast, but her mind and soul felt vindicated and satisfied. She was too busy to even notice that there was more than one set of eyes on her.

She made her way to her godmother's car. She'd taken it the day she found her body. She didn't plan on keeping it because she was sure she'd be found out quickly if she started driving it around. She drove toward the front of the cemetery and waited for the silver car. As soon as she saw it approaching, she ducked down to make sure the driver or passenger didn't notice her.

Lobo's driver pulled his Infiniti QX80 to the curb in front of their house. Giselle was busy looking at herself in her compact mirror. The explosion at the cemetery had startled her and she was checking her face to make sure she didn't have any major cuts. Her face was stinging from the dirt and little pebbles that flew into her face when the bomb went off.

Lobo was behaving like nothing had happened. He was on his phone taking a business call. Lobo's driver was the first to exit the SUV. He nodded at the car behind the SUV as if to say the coast was clear. The driver opened the back door on the side where Giselle sat so that she could exit first. As soon as Giselle put her second foot out of the door and onto the ground, loud cracking noises erupted around her.

"Agh!" Giselle screamed and tried to duck back into the SUV, but it was too late. The noises seemed to get closer and closer until Giselle could hear nothing else. Somewhere in the distance she thought she could hear Lobo calling out to her.

Bullets rained down on the SUV. Giselle was hit at least four times. Her body jerked like she was being hit with bolts of electricity. Finally, her limp form slid out of the back passenger's side door onto the cold concrete.

Inside the vehicle, Lobo had tried to dive to the front of the vehicle, but the bullets had penetrated the doors and hit him two times; it was the bullet to the side of face that had finally taken his life. His body was slumped over, leaning awkwardly on the center console.

The driver lay on the street next to Giselle and the security guard who had been sitting in the front passenger's seat lay between the front seats, bleeding from his head. In the second vehicle the driver was slumped over the steering wheel. The horn was now blaring from his dead body weight pressing down on it. The two men who had tried to escape from the back doors were each riddled with bullets and hanging halfway out of the doors.

Tiana threw her godmother's M60 fully automatic machine gun in the trunk, got in the car, and calmly drove away like nothing had ever happened. Within minutes screams erupted on the streets from the sight. The 911 lines were jammed with calls and in no time the wail of police sirens could be heard in the distance.

Chapter 18

While Drake was slumped on the couch in Tiana's apartment sound asleep, Tiana did one of his moves. She crept out of her bed and out of the apartment without waking him. With her gun in her waist and two knives stuck in her small knapsack, Tiana set out on a mission.

An hour later, Tiana stood inside of Quality Monument, a grave monument store on Fenton Road. She was viewing headstones for Mama Hilda's grave. Tiana didn't care if she had to spend all that remained of the money from her war bag; she wasn't going to let Mama Hilda rest in an unmarked grave. She wanted to buy the headstone before one of Mama Hilda's relatives had the chance. Tiana felt like it was the least she could do.

"These are the most expensive ones," said a saleswoman as she walked up on Tiana. The woman's eyebrow was raised like she was warning rather than telling Tiana about the prices.

"It's okay. These are the ones I want to pick from," Tiana replied with an attitude as she ran her hand over a beautiful, shiny black onyx headstone floor sample.

"If you say so," the woman said, raising both of her eyebrows this time. "Well, here is the book with those styles. You can view it and pick something out," the woman said, leading Tiana to a small, round table at the back of the store. Just then the door chimes sounded at the front door, indicating that another customer had arrived. The saleswoman quickly turned her attention from Tiana to the door.

"Excuse me," the saleswoman said, rushing to the customer who'd entered like anyone would be more important than Tiana.

"Good afternoon." The voice came from Tiana's right, but it caught her attention like it was directed toward her. Tiana snapped her head up quickly and looked toward the front of the store. Her breath caught in her throat for a few quick seconds. *Oh, shit! That's him!* Tiana said to herself. She could never forget that familiar deep baritone voice. Tiana watched as the source of the voice moved farther into the store. Her suspicions had been correct. His face was one she would never forget. Tiana had thought about him from time to time since the night she'd run into him at the club, but she had figured that she'd most likely never see him again.

The guy who was the source of the familiar voice was busy speaking to the saleswoman, but Tiana was watching him from the corner of her eye. Seeing him standing in bright, natural sunlight he was even more gorgeous than she remembered. Just like the first time she'd seen him, he was well dressed again, but this time donning a sleek pair of designer jeans, a pair of black suede Giuseppe Zanotti sneakers, and a neat, fitted leather jacket. Tiana had to admit, Drake had nothing on this man when it came to looks and swag.

"I'm sorry for the loss of your loved one. You can view our books right over here," the saleswoman said, leading the guy to a table opposite the one Tiana was sitting at.

Tiana lowered her head and stole furtive glances at him. She didn't think he'd recognize her because the night she encountered him in Club Caliente she had her hair down and was dressed to the nines. Today, she had her hair pulled back in a ponytail, and wore a fitted black T-shirt and a dark blue pair of Gap skinny jeans.

"Did you find anything that fits your price point?" the saleswoman asked, coming up from behind and startling Tiana, who had gotten lost in her thoughts.

"Um, um, yeah, I saw one or two," Tiana stuttered, her cheeks flaming over when she noticed the man look over in her direction. *Damn, is he looking at me? Will he recognize me?* Tiana could feel the heat of the sexy man's gaze on her once again. Fine beads of sweat lined up at her hairline and she curled her toes up in her shoes.

Shit! He's staring now!

This schoolgirl crush behavior had her upset with herself. Tiana didn't like the fact that she was feeling another person this much without knowing anything about him. It was something she always tried to fight but her attraction to this guy was hard to ignore.

"Well, then, can I start an order for you? Was this your parent or close relative?" the annoying saleswoman pressed, breaking Tiana's train of thought.

"My godmother," Tiana replied dryly. "I kind of like this black and gray one right here." Tiana pointed to the book, trying to keep the hovering saleswoman off her back. Out of the corner of her eye, Tiana could see the guy getting up and coming in her direction. A hot feeling came over her and her hands quickly became clammy with sweat. She wrung them together under the table.

"Excuse me. I don't mean to interrupt, but have we met?" the gorgeous stranger interrupted the chattering saleswoman. Tiana and the saleswoman both turned their sights to the man with confusion ruffling their brows. Noticing the disapproving glare the saleswoman shot in his direction, he took a few steps back from the table where Tiana sat.

"I'm sorry." The guy looked at the saleswoman. Then he turned all of his attention to Tiana. "I didn't mean to interrupt. Trust me, I know this can be a hard thing to do, but I think we met at Caliente a few weeks ago. Remember? I'm the 'Can I buy you a drink might've gotten you somewhere' guy," the gorgeous man reminded her.

Tiana felt the heat of embarrassment climbing her neck and rising to her face. "Oh, okay, I think I kind of remember." Tiana played it off like she suddenly had a flash of recall.

"Wow, what a coincidence. This is a weird place to meet again. Maybe it's a sign," the man said, smiling awkwardly. "I'm Silam," he said, extending his hand. The saleswoman's mouth hung open slightly like she couldn't believe what was taking place.

"Cali," Tiana lied, taking his hand in hers and shaking it firmly. She took another good look at the man and butterflies flitted through her stomach. Those dark curls hugging his scalp, that smooth caramel skin, those deep-set eyes, and the tiny cleft in his chin had Tiana swooning.

"Did you lose someone close?" he asked Tiana, looking down at the thick binder filled with headstone pictures in front of her.

"My godmother," Tiana answered evasively. "Cancer." The lie rolled off her tongue as easily and fluidly as water down a stream.

"Sorry to hear that. For me, it was my brother," Silam said somberly. "A car fire."

"I hate to break up this little connection," the saleswoman interjected rudely, wedging herself between Tiana and Silam. "I just wanted to know if either of you are interested in starting an order," she continued.

Tiana shot the woman an evil look and let out a grunt. Suddenly, Tiana didn't want to give the woman her business. "I'll think about it and come back. For now, I'm just going to take two bouquets of the daisies with the grave stands," Tiana said, pointing to the front of the store.

"Yeah, I think I'll do the same," Silam said, smiling at Tiana like they'd just made a new alliance of some kind.

The flustered saleswoman stomped to the front of the store where the grave flowers were on display. She grumbled her dissatisfaction, causing Tiana and Silam to look at each other and chuckle. That was a first for Tiana; she'd let her guard down and it had taken almost nothing.

"So, since we met twice by what I'd like to refer to as fate, I think I would be dumb if I didn't ask for your number," Silam said, his words crisp and polite. "I definitely think we should stay in touch."

Tiana could tell right away he wasn't the average street dude she was used to. "I don't have a number, but I'll take yours," Tiana told him. Another lie that came out of her mouth with no hesitation.

"In this day and age a beautiful woman like you without a cell phone. C'mon, ma, I can't believe that," Silam said, twisting his lips in disbelief.

Tiana blushed again for the tenth time since Silam walked into the store. "Let's just say I'm different," Tiana replied sassily. "I don't do what every other girl in this day and age is doing."

Silam shook his head and laughed. "I hear that. Fair enough, tough girl. I forgot how tough you were that night in the club, but now I remember how you almost cut me for touching your arm." He laughed again.

"For the record, you didn't just touch. You grabbed it." Tiana chuckled and shifted her weight from one foot to the other. She didn't even realize that she was blushing. "And call it what you want. I bet next time you about to touch a chick in a club you'll remember me." They both erupted in laughter.

Silam jotted his number down on the back of one of the annoying saleswoman's cards and extended it toward Tiana. "This is a little old school, collecting numbers on paper, but I guess it's kind of romantic," he said.

Tiana took the card and examined the phone number for a few minutes. Her insides were doing all sorts of flips and jerks, but she played it cool. "A'ight, I got it," she said.

"Just promise me you're going to call it," Silam said, flashing his beautiful smile.

"I don't make promises, but I will make sure to give you a call," Tiana replied.

"I guess tough girls don't make promises. I guess I'll have to take what I can get. I hope we can get to know one another sooner rather than later, Cali," Silam told her.

"We'll see. Whatever is meant to be will be, right?" Tiana answered.

Silam raised his hands in front of him. "You got that," he said in playful surrender. "You win, tough girl."

"I always win," Tiana said, grabbing the flower bouquets and heading for the door.

"Not always," Silam said under his breath as he watched her leave. "Not always."

Silam left the store and walked half a block to where his driver patiently waited for him.

"Any luck? Was it her?" his driver asked.

"More than luck. I just hit the fucking jackpot."

Chapter 19

With her mind swirling with thoughts of Silam, Tiana decided she needed a distraction. She took a cab to Drake's house. She knew by then he would've been gone from her apartment. Lately, he was always at her house, so Tiana decided to surprise him. She kind of felt guilty about sneaking out on him and even more guilty about how attracted she was to this dude Silam.

"Your ass better be home, Drake," Tiana mumbled as she exited the cab. "I need you to get my mind right so I can get back in the damn game. I got a few more people to see."

Tiana climbed the stoop in front of Drake's building but, instead of knocking, she used the set of keys he'd given her for emergencies. She usually didn't carry the keys but, for some reason, today she had slid them into the front pocket of her knapsack.

Once Tiana was in the building's hallways she could hear music coming from Drake's apartment. She smiled. She was glad to learn that he was home.

Tiana put several more keys into the locks on Drake's apartment door and as she entered the apartment the music seemed uncomfortably loud. She paused for a few seconds, her eyebrows dipping low on her face.

"Why the fuck is he blasting love songs so loud?" Tiana whispered as she went farther into the apartment. The sound of Trey Songz filled the entire apartment. That wasn't Drake's usual choice of a playlist; he was the hardest hip-hop head Tiana knew.

"Drake!" she called out. She knew if he was in his bedroom he wouldn't be able to hear her. After a few seconds of standing still and waiting for him to answer, Tiana headed to his bedroom. When she got to the door, she could hear what sounded like voices mixing with the music.

Oh, Lord, this man is seriously talking to himself. Tiana giggled to herself as she turned the knob. "Locked bedroom door?" Tiana whispered. Her face was folded in confusion. She placed her ear up against the door. The sounds coming from inside struck her like an open-handed slap to the face.

Tiana could decipher the passionate noises from the music now. She heard a woman calling out Drake's name in ecstasy loud and clear now. Tiana's breathing became labored. The heat of anger began rising from her feet, climbing up into her chest. Then, as if possessed by a demon, and with her chest heaving up and down like it was being pumped up with a foot pump, Tiana kicked in Drake's bedroom door so hard it almost flew off the hinges.

"Ahh!" the woman inside screeched, jumping up from riding Drake. The woman tried in vain to cover her naked body with her hands. "Drake, what's going on?" the woman exclaimed, clearly shaken up.

"What the fuck?" Drake panted, springing to his feet. "Yo, Tiana, what you doing here?" he gasped, his dick still hard and seemingly taunting Tiana.

Tiana felt like a heavyweight championship boxer had just punched her in the gut. She couldn't even get the words out, but the heat that engulfed her body was enough to set the whole apartment on fire.

Drake recognized the fire flashing in Tiana's eyes and he noticed that she was biting down on her bottom lip so hard it was starting to bleed. He knew he had to do something quick. He came forward with his hands out in front of him pleadingly. "Tee, wait," he said apprehensively. "Let me explain."

Tiana reached behind her back and pulled out the gun she always carried on her. She raised her Glock and quickly screwed the silencer on to it. Before Drake could say another word, Tiana tugged back on the trigger and shot the girl in the arm. The girl squealed like a stuck pig and doubled over in pain. Tiana didn't even care where the bullet had struck the girl.

"Oh, shit! Tiana! What the fuck are you doing?" Drake hollered, terror etched on his face.

Tiana leveled her gun at Drake next. White hot, angry tears welled up in the backs of Tiana's eyes and her gun hand wavered unsteadily.

"C'mon, you can't shoot me. I'm your fucking best friend. I love—" he started.

"Don't you fucking say those words to me!" Tiana screamed, her finger moving to the trigger. Drake snapped his mouth shut with the quickness.

"Stay the fuck away from me, Drake! I never want to see you again. You lying motherfucker! I believed you when you said you loved me! I fucking trusted you with everything!" Tiana screamed as a hard lump painfully lodged in the back of her throat.

Tiana turned swiftly to leave. She knew if she stayed another second she would have the blood of her best friend on her hands.

"Wait! I do love you! Let me explain! I was trying to cut her off and tell her that I wanted to be with you!" Drake screamed as her ran after Tiana.

"You motherfucker! You better not leave me like this! That bitch is going to jail! Aghhh!" the girl started screaming.

Drake stood in the middle of the floor, caught between Tiana and the girl. He could feel his heart breaking.

"Well, now you don't have to tell the bitch nothing. I'll be out of your place in two days. Have a nice fucking life, Drake," Tiana said with the same eerily calm voice she spoke in each time she took down her marks.

"Wait!" she heard him scream after her.

Tiana raced down Drake's front steps with tears running down her face like a waterfall. The tears were more angry than tears of hurt. She couldn't believe that she'd let Drake convince her to cross the line, only to have him stomp all over her heart. Here she was feeling guilty about flirting and getting another guy's number, while Drake was straight up fucking somebody else. The pain she felt sizzled into a ball of fury that she needed to get rid of. She had more people on her list to see and with the rage roiling on her insides this was the perfect time to get back to it. She unfolded her list and read the next name listed on it. It was time for her to get her revenge on some assholes from Rollins.

Tiana read the address again to make sure she had the right place. The red brick two-story building looked run-down and decrepit, surely not a place she expected a doctor's administrative assistant to live. Tiana didn't have to use any special skills to get inside because the beat-up front door sat propped open by a milk crate with a dirty pillow on top of it.

Tiana had to kick through empty beer bottles, potato chip bags, and dirty food cartons to get to the stairs leading up to the second floor. The stench of burning hair, cat piss, and old grease assailed her nose when she got to the top. *Some nasty motherfuckers living in here.*

Tiana knocked on the door. She had her fake sales pitch line all ready in her head. After a few second she heard movement inside the apartment.

"Didn't I tell your ass not to forget—" Dana Shaw cussed as she yanked the door open. Her words were quickly cut short when Tiana placed the barrel of her .357 Sig Sauer on Dana's forehead.

"Don't fucking scream or your neighbors will find your brains all over the floor when they come home," Tiana growled, moving forward.

Dana shook her head up and down as she walked backward into the apartment. Tiana kept her gun pressed on Dana's forehead as she locked the door behind her.

"Never thought you'd see me again, huh?" Tiana grinned wickedly.

"Pl . . . please," Dana stuttered. Her teeth chattered together loudly like she was standing in an icy pile of snow with no clothes on.

"I think I remember saying please to you all of the times you arranged for my sessions to turn into rape and sodomy," Tiana gritted.

"I ha . . . had no choice," Dana cried, quickly realizing what was happening. "Please, I was only doing what I was told so I could feed my kids," she pleaded. Tiana lifted her gun and slammed it down on the bridge of Dana's nose.

"Agh! Oh, God!" Dana shrieked, throwing her hands up to protect her face. Blood gushed from her nose like a faucet turned on full blast. "Oh, God!" she screamed when she brought her bloodied hand eyelevel.

Tiana looked around and saw a bunch of toys thrown all throughout the floor, and sippy cups on a coffee table. "You set up the rape and sodomy of young girls to feed your kids?" Tiana growled, her nostrils flaring. She hit Dana again; this time the skin on Dana's forehead divided into a deep fleshy gash. Dana yelped like a wounded animal and fell backward onto the floor.

"Now don't fuck with me," Tiana growled. "I'm not here to play games. Get the fuck up and sit in the chair."

"Okay," Dana managed, easing herself up from the floor and down in one of her rickety kitchen chairs. Blood and tears made a mess of her face. She hung her head, scared to look at Tiana.

"Give me some information and I might let you live. I need to know where Teema Chambers lives," Tiana demanded, grabbing a handful of Dana's hair and forcing her head up until she was looking her in the eyes.

"I don't know. She never filled out the same paperwork as everyone else," Dana whimpered. Tiana brought her gun across Dana's face again.

"Agh!" Dana screamed. This time she felt her cheekbone collapse under her skin. "I swear. Teema had some special arrangements with the doctor. I never asked about it. But, I have something else. I have something that might help you," Dana said pleadingly, just wanting the beating to stop.

"Something else like what?" Tiana growled, her gun hanging over Dana's head.

"I have the key to a safe deposit box. I took everything out of the one Dr. Syed had after he was killed and I put it all into a new one in my name. Inside there's plenty of money, paperwork, and other stuff. It . . . it might help you find Teema," Dana rambled in a desperate attempt to save her own life.

"Where's the key?" Tiana asked.

"My purse. Over there." Dana pointed.

"What bank?"

"Chase Bank. The one on Flushing Road."

Tiana put her gun to Dana's head and grabbed her arm, forcing Dana up from the chair. "Move slow and don't try no bullshit," Tiana warned. "I don't care about spilling your fucking brains in here."

Dana shook her head left to right saying no. She sobbed as Tiana led her to her purse.

"Tell me where in the purse. I don't trust you to dig for it," Tiana snarled.

"The small pocket inside. It's the little gold key on the hospital keychain," Dana told her.

With one hand holding her gun on Dana, Tiana used her other hand to fish around in the purse. She located the key and stuffed it into her pocket.

Dana's eyes went wide. "Please. I have kids. They don't have anyone else to take care of them. I never agreed with what he did to y—"

Two shots to the head ended Dana's sentence before she could finish it.

"This is not personal; it's vengeance. Y'all all never agreed with what he did but you bitches just never tried to stop it, never called the cops, never did shit to help us," Tiana said to Dana's corpse.

Chapter 20

Tiana went back to the small motel that she'd been staying in since she'd fallen out with Drake. She didn't want to stay at the apartment he had gotten for her anymore because she didn't want him to know where she was. Since that day she caught Drake with the other girl, she had only gone to the apartment once to get the bag her dad had left and a few changes of clothes.

Once she was in her motel room she unpacked her bag and thought about her next move. As she finished emptying her bag she saw what looked like a business card fall and hit her foot. Tiana let out a long sigh when she looked down and saw the card with Silam's phone number on it.

"You again?" Tiana mumbled. She had been toying with the idea of calling Silam for a few days now, but each time Tiana thought about starting something with another man, she would let fear of being hurt again take over her mind, and she put it out of her mind immediately.

Now, she stared at the card contemplating hard whether she should just step out on faith and call. Tiana was lonely and the one thing most people didn't know about her was that she hated being lonely.

Tiana bent down and picked up the card. She stared at the curly handwriting for a few minutes and read the numbers over and over until she almost had them memorized.

"Your ass gonna just keep popping up everywhere anyway," Tiana said, plucking the card with her middle finger. "Maybe it is meant to be." With that, she twisted her lips, tilted her head slightly, and let go of her fears.

"Fuck it. If I don't like you, I'll just add you to my list," she said, half joking, half serious. She sat down on the side of the bed, picked up the motel phone, and dialed the number. When Silam picked up, Tiana flopped back on the bed with a huge smile on her face, happy that he wasn't able to see how happy she was that he'd answered.

Tiana looked at herself one more time in the dull, scratched-up mirror hanging over the bathroom sink. "Can't see shit," she grumbled as she leaned closer to apply another coat of the cheap Revlon lipstick she had copped from CVS. She smacked her lips together and stood back to examine herself again.

"A nigga got you wearing makeup, tight-ass jeans, and uncomfortable-ass heels. You're a sucker for good-looking men, bitch," Tiana scolded herself, then smiled. Tiana had depended on the salesgirl at the mall to help her pick out something that would look dressy enough, but wouldn't make her look like she wasn't trying too hard. The girl had recommended a simple pair of dark, distressed Joe's Jeans, a fitted Romeo & Juliet T-shirt, and a pair of nude pointed-toe pumps. The outfit had come together well.

Tiana turned around and examined herself from the back. She shook her head up and down. She didn't think she looked too bad. Celeste would've been proud of her for the ensemble. Tiana thought she could get used to this girlie stuff. She liked to dress up every now and then to show the feminine side of herself.

Tiana rushed out of the bathroom and peered over at the motel's digital clock. She had about fifteen minutes to make it to the Genesee Valley Center mall parking lot where she had told Silam to meet her. Tiana threw her Glock into the royal blue suede, fringed pocketbook she had bought, and she headed out of the door.

"Shit!" Tiana cursed as her cab slowed to a stop. She'd spotted Silam in the parking lot posted up outside of his car. "This nigga here already." Tiana shook her head. She didn't want him to see her getting out of a cab, but it was too late now. Her nerves had all of the hairs on her body standing at attention. She gave herself a pep talk as she walked over to where Silam stood looking fine as hell as usual.

"You always stand outside of your car in the middle of a mall parking lot looking like a creep?" Tiana joked as she approached. Silam flashed his perfect smile. Tiana's heartbeat sped up. *This dude is fine as shit!*

"Nah, I just wanted to make sure I didn't miss my beautiful date," Silam said, taking in an eyeful of Tiana's beauty and swag.

Tiana blushed. *Get it together, bitch! He's a man, just a man!*

Silam walked around to the passenger's side door of his black Mercedes S550 and opened the door for Tiana.

"Why did I already figure out that you drove this kind of car?" Tiana said as she slid into the dark gray leather seat.

Silam walked around and got in on his side. "What does that mean?" he asked, chuckling.

"I don't know. You just seem like the S550 type of dude and before I got here something told me you drove an S550. I guess it was intuition," Tiana replied.

"Shit, I hope that means your intuition is telling you I'm the type of dude who likes the finer things in life, including the beautiful woman I got sitting next to me," he said, laying his corny game on.

Tiana shrugged and shifted uncomfortably in her seat. Silam had her insides feeling all mushy.

"I got a special night planned for us, Cali," Silam said as he pulled his car out of the parking lot.

Tiana wore a goofy smile. She was definitely out of her element. She also had her guard down dangerously low. So low, she never noticed the two cars trailing behind them.

Three weeks after their first date Tiana and Silam were inseparable. He had taken her on two lavish shopping sprees and each time they were together he presented her with a different luxury gift. So far, Tiana had collected a Cartier watch with a double row of diamonds on the bezel, a pair of five-carat diamond solitaire earrings, and a new iPhone so that Silam could stay in touch with her when they were apart. Things were moving at a speed Tiana couldn't control, but Silam was such a welcomed distraction from the hurt, death, and destruction she was used to that Tiana went along for the ride without hesitation. She had decided to put her plans to the side and just enjoy herself with Silam for a little bit.

"So this is it," Silam announced, opening his arms wide. Tiana's mouth hung open slightly as she whirled around on the balls of her feet. The sight was breathtaking. Forget the luxurious place Silam lived in with all of its expensive furnishings. Tiana was enamored with something else.

"Damn, this is gorgeous," Tiana said in awe. "This view is everything. This shit is giving me life right now," she gasped, rushing over to the long wall of floor-to-ceiling windows. Tiana looked out at the city in amazement like a little kid staring at the biggest roller coaster at an amusement park. She felt like she was on top of the world standing in Silam's place.

"I'm glad you like it," Silam said, walking over to share the view of the city with her. "I'm glad you agreed to come home with me, too," he said sexily. "It only took three weeks to get you here." He laughed.

Tiana's pulse quickened. The sexual tension between the two of them was palpable, to say the least. They hadn't done more than some hot and heavy kissing up until that moment, but both of their minds were on doing more.

"What?" Silam asked, noticing the strain on her face.

"Nothing. Nothing. I'm good," Tiana lied, moving closer to him. She was thinking about Drake and how badly he'd hurt her. Revenge was what drove most of her actions and this wasn't going to be any different. Tiana wanted to know that she could have someone else just like Drake had.

With thoughts of revenge controlling her actions, Tiana reached up, grabbed Silam's head and pulled him close to her face. He took the signal and leaned his tall frame down to meet her. Tiana parted her lips and allowed his tongue into her mouth. She sucked on it softly, which caused her pussy to pulse. Silam gently placed his hands on each side of her face and steadied her head as they kissed passionately. Tiana moved her body against his, feeling his muscular chest against her erect nipples. Within a few minutes she could also feel his iron-stiff erection pressing against the top of her pelvis.

"Damn, you feel so good," Silam whispered in her ear. A hot feeling tingled through Tiana's body. She wasn't going to fight it this time. She wanted to be feminine. She wanted to be sexy. Most of all, she just wanted to be wanted.

Silam grabbed her hand and led her through his beautiful penthouse apartment. Tiana wasn't being observant. She wasn't doing her usual scan for the nearest exits or for things she could use as weapons just in case she needed them. Tiana's head was swimming with lust and she let it take over all of her good sense.

Tiana eased down onto Silam's bed and he climbed on top of her. They shared more deep, passionate kisses. Tiana made the first move and hoisted Silam's shirt up.

Silam took the cue and leaned up so Tiana could remove his shirt. He smiled down at her. It was a weird smile, part wicked, part sensual. Tiana leaned up and ran her hands slowly over the curves of his perfect muscular chest and his six-pack abs.

"Damn," she huffed. "You're perfect."

"Nah, far from perfect," he said, his voice gruff with lust.

Tiana moved from under Silam and signaled for him to lie down. He complied. She stood in front of him and let her inhibitions fall away. She slowly lifted her tight-fitting T-shirt over her head and quickly unsnapped her bra. Her breasts sat up taut and perky, seemingly winking at Silam and urging him on. Tiana's hair fell over her shoulders and covered parts of breasts enough to give them a sexy mystique.

"Shit. You're fucking sexy," he whispered. He was losing himself in her aura. This wasn't part of the plan but he was following his feelings just like Tiana was. Plans and calculations were all tossed away at that moment.

Tiana slowly shimmied her hips side to side until her jeans were off. She left her sexy black lace panties on, figuring she would leave Silam something to remove. Without a word, Tiana climbed onto the bed, pushed Silam down, and leaned over him. *You can do this, Tiana. You can be what a man wants,* she told herself as she began licking his neck. She arched her back and slithered a little farther down, trailing her tongue down to his pecks and gently biting the right one.

"Sss," Silam hissed in pleasure. The slurping noises and his reactions were like batteries in Tiana's back. She continued down his abdomen, taking special care to run her tongue over every ridge on his sexy, firm six pack. Silam groaned. When Tiana got to his belt line, she inched back and looked up at his face. She parted a mischievous smile and bit her bottom lip seductively.

Tiana loosened Silam's belt, unzipped his pants, and dug for the treasure she was hunting for. Silam let out a long puff of air and whispered something but Tiana couldn't make out what he'd said. It didn't matter because she wasn't going to stop until she got what she wanted.

Tiana grabbed on to Silam's rock-hard rod and ran her hand up and down over it. Silam closed his eyes and grunted in ecstasy. He couldn't take the teasing any longer. He sat up and flipped Tiana over onto her back before she could even react or protest.

"Wait," she whispered. A pang of fear flitted through her chest. She didn't like the feeling of being overpowered. It would make her have memories and she was trying to keep them away.

"Shhh," he said. Silam kissed her stomach as he inched down and pulled her panties off. He looked Tiana in the eye and put her panties up to his nose and sniffed them. "Mmmm," he moaned.

Tiana's chest rose and fell in anticipation of what was coming. Silam slid a condom on. He used his knee to gently part her legs. Tiana lifted her knees willingly to help him.

Silam slowly guided his manhood into her deep, wet center. Tiana let out a song of soft moans and groans as he ground into her.

"Oh," she cooed. He felt so good. They fit together perfectly.

"Gotdamn!" Silam belted out, picking up speed from the excitement of feeling her tightness grab on to him. Tiana dug her nails into the skin on his back, letting him know he was hitting it right. After a few minutes, she urged him up off of her.

"Let me ride it," she panted. Silam quickly lay down on his back. Tiana climbed over his stiff tool and lowered herself down on it.

"Ohhh," she called out as it penetrated her insides until she felt like it was in her guts. Silam put his hands on her waist and guided her up and down. Tiana quickly grasped his rhythm and began bouncing on his thick pole.

"Oh, shit!" she yelled. "Oh, shit!" Tiana had never felt the explosive feeling she was experiencing right then. Not even with Drake. *This must be what an orgasm feels like.* The feeling made her bounce up and down on Silam harder and faster.

"Yeah," he growled, clutching two handfuls of her ass cheeks. Tiana rocked back and forth and then swirled her hips. The movement caused Silam's pubic hairs to rub ever so slightly against Tiana's clitoris. The combination of deep penetration and the slight touches on her clit made Tiana explode.

"Ahhhh! Ahhhh!" she screamed out. She clutched on to Silam's shoulders as her body bucked. Small fireworks exploded in her head and squirms of light filled her eyesight. Tiana didn't want the good feeling that flooded her body to stop. She rocked harder and faster now. She leaned down slightly just enough for Silam to be able to lick her rock-hard nipples. Another explosion erupted in her loins.

"Ahhhhh!" Tiana belted out. Her entire body shook and all of a sudden she was weak. Her legs trembled fiercely and she simply couldn't move her waist anymore. Tiana was spent. It was only a few seconds later that Silam's body tensed up and he yelled, "I'm about to bust!"

Tiana collapsed on top of Silam as they both tried to calm their rapid breathing. She closed her eyes and decided that this was right where she was supposed to be. Maybe it was meant to be. She had repeated that line several times since they'd started seeing each other. She kept trying to convince herself that what she had with Silam wasn't too good to be true. Problem was, she wasn't being fully honest with telling him who she really was. Tiana had no idea how she was going to eventually tell him the truth.

Chapter 21

In the weeks Tiana had been spending with Silam, she had lost track of all her plans. Their whirlwind love had been a welcomed distraction for Tiana. Silam had treated her almost as good as her father had when she was a little girl. There was nothing she asked Silam for that he didn't make happen. He'd even taken her on a romantic trip to New York City. Ever since they'd gotten back, though, something in Tiana's gut told her she needed to get her head out of the clouds.

Under protest from Silam, Tiana decided she had to go back to the apartment Drake had let her stay in so she could gather the rest of her things and figure out what she was going to do next. As cloudy as her head was, Tiana wasn't sure if she had it in her to continue her streak of revenge killings.

After a bunch of back and forth and pleading for Tiana to just forget about her stuff and just move in with him, Silam relented and hired a car service to drop her off.

As soon as Tiana exited the black Lincoln Town Car, she spotted Drake's car parked outside of the building. She let out a long sigh. *I knew this nigga would be lurking and looking for me. He probably been here every day since I been gone. Bastard. Some fucking nerve.* She was trying to mentally prepare herself to see Drake without jumping on him and scratching his eyes out. He was already lucky she hadn't shot his dick off that day.

Tiana entered the apartment, readying herself for the bullshit she was sure Drake would be kicking. She dug inside her bag, pulled her gun out, and put it on her waist. She didn't trust Drake anymore. Period.

"Drake?" Tiana called out. "I know you're in here. I saw your car outside and I'm not in the mood for your bullshit," Tiana shouted, heading into the kitchen. "I told you I never wanted to fucking see you again so I don't even know why you're here!" she continued. When she didn't get a response, she walked to the living room and pulled her gun from the holster.

Not again, Tiana thought, her heart running so fast she could barely keep her breathing steady.

"Drake? If you're in here, stop playing. You shouldn't even be here, much less playing fucking games," Tiana shouted. She slowly inched toward the bedroom with her gun in hand just in case.

As she got to the closed bedroom door, Tiana wondered why it was closed and why he wasn't responding. Watching the bottom of the door, Tiana noticed a slight change in light under the door. It was movement. *Fuck! Maybe it's not Drake!* she screamed in her head. Tiana began slowly backing down the hallway leading to the apartment's exit door.

Before she could make it to the door, her bedroom door swung open and thunderous footsteps came in her direction. Tiana instinctively raised her gun but the dark figure was barreling at her so fast she couldn't keep a good grip on it. Tiana didn't bother to try aiming again. She spun around and bolted for the door.

"Ugh," she grunted as the weight of the person came crashing down on her right before she could get all of the locks undone on the door. Tiana's gun fell from her shaking hand and skittered across the floor as she fell forward.

"Agh!" she cried. "Get the fuck off me!" Tiana squirmed and kicked.

"Stop! Stop! I'm not going to fucking hurt you, Tiana!" Drake screamed.

"Get the fuck off of me!" she yelled back, flipping onto her back and swatting at his face. "Why are you chasing me down like that? What kind of fucking stupid-ass game are you playing!"

"Ouch! Fuck!" He winced, grabbing his cheek. Tiana had caught him good and dug a deep scratch into his left cheek. "Yo, you are fucking crazy and dangerous! You was just going to try to bust shots out without checking for who it is," Drake spat, holding his face.

"Didn't I fucking tell you to leave me the fuck alone? You lucky I didn't get a good grip and blast on your ass," Tiana growled, slowly pulling herself up off the floor. "Get the fuck out anyway. Oh, wait, I forgot this is your place. You don't have to leave. I'm fucking leaving," she barked at him. Tiana started gathering up her things.

"Wait! Wait a fucking minute! I just need you to fucking listen to me for once in your life, Tiana," Drake said. He stood in her way so she had to listen to him. "I've been staying here ever since the day we had our fight. I have some important shit to say and I need you to listen."

"I don't care what you have to fucking say!" Tiana barked, limping over and picking up her gun from the floor.

"So you're still mad and I get that. What happened at my apartment was definitely my fault. I said I was sorry and I mean that shit. I'ma take the L on that one. I was trying to cut the bitch off, but I had a few too many drinks and she took advantage of me," Drake confessed.

Tiana squinted her eyes at him. "You can't be fucking serious right now with that fuck boy story," Tiana retorted. "She just held you down and put your dick up in her pussy, right? So you're saying she forced you to fuck her ? Tuh, yeah, right. Didn't look like that to me," Tiana spat. He was so lucky she had years and years of love for him or else she would've had no problem spilling his brains for what he had done to her heart.

"I know it sounds like a dog nigga's story, but it's the truth. I have loved your ass since we were kids. Why would you think I would purposely hurt you like that? I didn't expect shit to go the way it did," he explained. "You just don't know how bad I want to be with you, Tee," he said, softening his voice. "I've been here every day for the past couple of weeks looking for you. I was scared I was never gonna see you again. I been staying here hoping you'd come back eventually," he said with regret in his words.

Mentally and physically exhausted, Tiana flopped down on the couch. It was hard for her to resist her best friend's sorry voice. She leaned her head back and closed her eyes. She had to stay focused. Drake sounded like he was being sincere; but, at the same time, she wasn't sure if she could really trust what he was saying. She started thinking about Silam. Then she started thinking about Mama Hilda. Then she started thinking maybe it was time for her to get back to her list. Her mind was going a mile a minute.

"Look, Drake, I don't know what to make of all this. For real. I got a lot going on," Tiana said.

"Tee, I want to fucking be with you more than anything in the world. Shit, I'm risking my life by talking to you right now," Drake said sincerely.

"What do you mean?" Tiana asked. His last statement confused her.

"Did you blow up a car that belonged to a Dr. Syed?" Drake asked her.

Tiana was taken aback by his question. She really hadn't expected that at all. "Yes, I did." She was a little hesitant to admit it.

Drake looked down to the ground and began to shake his head. He pursed his lips and took a deep breath through his nose.

"How do you know I did that?" she asked him.

"Because that doctor was my boss's brother, Tee. And that little boy who was with him was his son."

Tiana gasped and brought her hands to her mouth. She couldn't believe the bomb Drake had just dropped on her.

"I told you before, Gates runs the fucking city. So you fucked around and killed the son and brother of the most dangerous motherfucker in the Midwest."

Tiana's eyes widened when he said the words "son" and "brother."

"Now, I don't know why you had a need to go and kill Gates's brother, but I know your ass is in a lot deeper than you thought. He put out a hundred stack bounty on your head."

Tiana let out a long sigh. She didn't know how to respond to the information.

"You have to get out of town as soon as possible," Drake said. "For real. This shit is all fucked up right now. If they found out I know you and I didn't tell them, I'm a goner."

Tiana considered everything Drake had told her. "Nah. I ain't leaving town. I'm not scared of no fucking kingpin. I have a few more people to see and then maybe I'll consider it; but, right now, I'm here to stay," Tiana said stubbornly, shaking her head left to right.

"You don't have to do all this shit anymore. You need to go off the grid for a while. I'm telling you, this dude S. Gates is out to get you and he ain't gonna stop. He has a lot of people looking for you and it won't be long before shit blows up." Drake did his best to try to convince her.

Tiana shook her head. "I love y'all for looking out, but some things I have to do alone," Tiana said flatly, leaving no more room for discussion. "If he got my name, that means he got the means to come find me, too. I can't wait to meet him."

Drake looked straight at Tiana and shook his head. They knew there was no winning with her. Once her mind was made up, there was no convincing her otherwise.

"You keep thinking you're ass is untouchable but, Tee, if you keep messing around it's all gonna catch up to you. Some of the baddest motherfuckers out there have messed with Gates and they're all six feet under now."

"I hear what you're saying, Drake, but I gotta do what I gotta do."

"A'ight. I guess there's nothing else I can say to change your mind. I can't be around you right now. They can't find out I know who you are. I'ma do my best to keep them from finding you," Drake promised with feeling.

"Thanks, Drake." They gave each other a hug and, with that, Drake left her to be alone in the apartment.

"You wanna come for me, motherfucker?" Tiana growled. "Bring it! Whoever the fuck you are! Bring it!"

Tiana scrambled through the apartment like a mad-woman collecting things she needed. When her war bag was filled she stopped, took a deep breath, and said three Hail Marys in Spanish. Tiana knew it was time for her to get back to her original plans.

Silam was going to have to be put on hold for now. She sent him a quick text saying that she needed to take some time to herself because things were moving too fast between them. She asked him not to respond and to just give her some time.

Chapter 22

Tiana rushed out of the Chase bank with her backpack secured tightly under her arm. Her heart raced wildly from being so nervous about posing as Dana Shaw to gain access to the safe deposit box. Tiana jumped into the cab she had paid to wait for her and instructed him to take her to her apartment. She needed to grab the computer Drake had lent her so she could look at the discs she retrieved from the safe deposit box. Tiana prayed silently that they held some clue as to where she could find the very last person on her list, Teema Chambers. After that, Tiana would look for this Gates guy and she would take care of him too.

Tiana paid the cab driver and rushed inside the building. Once she was inside the apartment, she dumped the contents of her knapsack out on the kitchen table.

"Fuck," she said breathlessly as she eyed the stacks of cash in front of her. She hadn't had enough time inside the bank to really take it all in. Tiana picked up two of the stacks, held them up to her nose, inhaled, and exhaled. She felt exhilarated by the scent of the money. When everything was done she was going to use some of the money to surprise Silam and take him to Jamaica for a much-needed getaway.

Tiana sifted through the other items. There was a huge diamond engagement ring that had a clear, sparkly emerald-cut center stone that looked to be at least five carats. There were also two Rolex watches with beautiful mother-of-pearl faces.

"Humph. His and hers?" Tiana examined the watches. Suddenly, she remembered that she'd seen the woman's watch on Teema at least once during her participating in Dr. Syed's sick acts.

"I gotta find this bitch," Tiana mumbled. She rushed to the living room and picked up Drake's laptop. Back at the table, Tiana retrieved the first disc and slid it into the side of the laptop.

Tiana clicked on a couple of the folders that popped up on the screen. Then she found one that said Recordings and she clicked on that one.

"No! Help me! Please!"

Tiana bit into the side of her cheek when she realized it was Celeste's voice on the first recording. Tiana squinted as the camera came into focus and she could see what was happening. Dr. Syed was walking slowly toward Celeste, who was bound to the bed, with a long black rubber object in his hand.

Tiana could hear Teema laughing in the background. Tiana quickly clicked out of the recording. She couldn't watch. There were at least ten other similar recordings of Tiana, Celeste, Elizabeth, and other female patients. In the last file, Tiana found something useful to her.

"Listen, you know that I can't leave him just like that," Teema cried.

"Oh, yeah? Well, how about I tell him whose son it is?" Dr. Syed replied.

"Why are you doing this all of a sudden?" Teema asked pleadingly.

"I'm tired of playing second fiddle to a street thug who thinks he runs the world. Fucking S. Gates. That fake bullshit thug name he calls himself. I've never been good enough compared to him. Look at me! I became a doctor and yet he still gets everything! Everyone still holds him in such high regard! I loved you from day one, but who do you marry? Him!" Dr. Syed growled.

"No. I always loved you. You know yourself why I married him. It was an arrangement my father made and I couldn't break it. Please, don't do this. He can never know about the baby. Please! He will kill both of us," Teema cried some more. "I will keep doing everything you ask me to do here, with these girls, the sex, the crazy, freaky things; just don't tell. I will be with you one day. We will be able to get away together. I just have to wait for the right time," she begged.

"I'm not going to keep up this lie for much longer, so you better work it out. You better make sure I am able to continue spending time alone with my son, too," Dr. Syed threatened.

Tiana's mouth hung open. "Ain't this about a bitch? Fucking Teema is married to S. Gates. So he does fucking exist. What a grimy bitch she is," Tiana said aloud, completely flabbergasted by what she had just learned.

Tiana replayed the recording of Dr. Syed and Teema at least ten times before the information settled in her mind. Teema was married to S. Gates who was also Dr. Syed's brother! Tiana watched two more of the discs and shook her head in disbelief at how Dr. Syed and Teema kept video of themselves and what they were doing to the girls in the hospital.

"I have to find this bitch Teema before Gates finds me. I wonder what he would do if he found out the truth, since he is supposed to be so dangerous," Tiana said to herself out loud.

Her phone buzzing on the kitchen table startled Tiana. She sucked her teeth and blew out a long breath when she saw that it was Drake.

"This nigga must have a GPS tracking device on my ass," Tiana mumbled as she picked up the line. "Hello," Tiana answered dryly.

Drake didn't bother with small talk. He was rambling too much and so fast, but Tiana understood everything that he was saying. She gripped the phone until her knuckles turned white as she listened to Drake.

"Tiana! He knows who you are and he knows where you're staying! Whatever you do, stay the fuck away from the apartment!"

Tiana's entire body turned cold, like someone had pumped ice water into her veins.

After the initial shock of what Drake said finally wore off, Tiana scrambled up from the table. She gathered the money, the jewelry, and the discs from the safe deposit box and slid them into her backpack. She grabbed her war bag and headed for the door. When she opened the door to step out, Tiana ran smack dead into someone.

"Oh, shit!" she gasped, her bladder almost emptying into her pants.

"What, you're not happy to see me?" Silam said with a sexy, sinister smile on his face.

Tiana's lips were white, like she'd just eaten a powered doughnut. Her heart slammed against her chest bone and fine beads of sweat cropped up at her hairline.

"How . . . What . . . what are you doing here?" Tiana managed.

"It was easy to find you. I just called my friend at the car service," Silam said.

Tiana was too caught up to even think to ask him how he knew what apartment to go to inside the building.

"Um, I have to go somewhere. Can I meet up with you later?" Tiana said, her words rushing out in quivery bursts.

"Where do you need to go? I'll take you. I'm not letting you get away this time," Silam said, grabbing Tiana's shaking hand.

She parted a nervous smile. She didn't know why she couldn't just tell Silam to get lost. She was feeling something for him that was definitely clouding her good judgment.

"Something's happened to my mother," Tiana said. "I have to go see about her," she lied.

"Oh, good. I would love to meet her," Silam pressed as they both stepped outside of her building.

Tiana stopped walking and pulled her hand away from Silam. "Look, Silam. I need to do this alone. I promise I will call you when I can," Tiana insisted.

Silam's face suddenly went dark and he lowered his eyes into slits. "I am not letting you get away from me this time. You need to come with me," Silam growled, grabbing on to her arm.

Tiana was taken aback by the change. "Get off me!" she snapped.

Just then a black van screeched to a halt in front of them. Silam smiled wickedly. Three men jumped out of the van. Silam pushed her toward them with a satisfied smirk painting his face.

"What the fuck?" Tiana huffed, her eyes going wide. She looked at Silam with desperation dancing over her face. It was too late. "What the fuck are you doing?" Tiana screamed as she stared into Silam's eyes.

"Your worst fucking nightmare," Silam said evenly. One of the men from the van threw a black bag over Tiana's head while the other two forced her, kicking and screaming, into the van.

"Take her to the warehouse," Silam said, picking up Tiana's knapsack and war bag from the street. He wasn't leaving any clues of her disappearance behind.

"Yes, Mr. Gates," the driver of the van answered.

Lying on the cold metal floor of the van, Tiana kicked and moved her body frantically.

"Keep fucking still before I tie your ass up," one of the men growled at her.

"Fuck you," Tiana spat. "Agh!" she cried out as a huge, booted foot slammed into her ribs. Tiana coughed, but she kept trying to fight. A punch landed to her face and she saw stars but Tiana still didn't stop fighting. Another one of the men got close to her and tried to get her tied up. Tiana moved so much the black hood covering her head came up slightly, but the man didn't see it in time.

"Argh!" the man belted out. Tiana had clamped her teeth down on his wrist and wouldn't let go. "Get the fuck off me, bitch!" he hollered. Tiana thrust her foot forward and caught the other man in the balls.

"Ooof!" he wheezed, rolling over onto his side.

"What the fuck is going on back there?" the driver screamed.

Tiana released her bite on the first man's wrist and blood covered her mouth. She struggled to get up, but the man she had kicked in the balls recovered and moved toward her.

"You fucking bitch!" he hissed, obviously still reeling from the pain.

Tiana squirmed helplessly. She had no more tricks left. Both men were well aware of what they were dealing with now. In pain and a little dazed, Tiana tried to roll as far away from them as she could. She was too slow and there was nowhere for her to run. The man she had bitten kneeled over her and slammed his gun against her right temple.

Bam! Tiana felt the pressure from the hit and everything immediately faded to black.

Chapter 23

When Tiana came into consciousness she heard the muffled sound of voices surrounding her. When she opened her eyes, she realized she couldn't see anything because the bag had been placed back on her. The pounding in her head was so bad even her teeth hurt.

"Mmm," she groaned, trying in vain to lift her head.

"She's awake!" a man announced loudly.

"Good. Bring her over here so she can see the mess she's made," a familiar voice echoed loudly through the hollow room.

"Ahh." Tiana winced. Pain shot through her rib cage as she was handled roughly. She was dragged to another part of the expansive warehouse. Before she could see it, the smell hit her like a kick to the chest and she gagged. It was a mixture of raw meat gone bad, burning flesh, shit, and piss. The bag was lifted off of her and she was finally able to see where she was. Standing right in front of her was Silam.

"Silam! What the fuck is going on?" she asked him.

"Please allow me to introduce myself," he said with a sinister smirk on his face. "I am Silam Gates."

Tiana's heart dropped and she felt like the oxygen had just been taken out of the room.

"What's the matter, baby? Cat got you tongue?" he asked her rhetorically. "That's right, you've been sleeping with the enemy this whole time. Talk about keeping your friends close and your enemies closer. You just took that phrase to a whole new level!" He erupted with laughter.

Tiana let her head drop low and just stared at the ground.

"Speaking of friends, you know him?" S. Gates asked, grabbing a handful of Tiana's hair and forcing her down-turned head to look upward.

"Drake!" she rasped. "No. No." Tiana shook her head as painful tears danced down her bruised cheeks. She couldn't even look at Drake's naked and bleeding body suspended by chains from a metal rafter. There was a piece of metal that resembled a horse bit forced with wires hanging from it between Drake's lips.

"Ohh, so you do know him," Gates said, amused. He nodded at his henchmen. One of them walked over to a small box that contained three levers. He flipped on the switches and pulled down the first lever.

"Grrrr! Grrrr! Agh!" Drake's body jerked and curled in response to the high jolts of electricity that hit him. Tiana heard some kind of liquid splashing on the floor and knew it was coming from Drake's body.

"Please! No! Stop!" Tiana begged, closing her eyes.

S. Gates let out a raucous, maniacal laugh. Tiana kept her eyes closed and her head down. Gates signaled his men to cut the electricity. Drake's body finally relaxed, but it swung limp and lifeless above Tiana's head.

"One more round of that and he won't make it," S. Gates said, smiling evilly at Tiana. "He rushed here like a hero to save you. Isn't that sweet? All of those months I was searching for you he tried to act like he didn't know who you were. Then, just like that, I find out you were hiding out with him right under my nose," he continued cruelly.

"Let him go," Tiana croaked through her battered lips. "It's me you want. Not him. I'm here. I'm not scared to die. Just let him go and kill me."

"I'll get to that but, first, I want you to see what it feels like to have those close to you suffer and die for no reason," S. Gates said through gritted teeth. "Now, open your fucking eyes and look at him before I gut him like a pig just like I did your godmother!"

Tiana slowly lifted her head with fire flashing in her eyes. Her hands involuntarily curled into fists. She looked up at Drake's limp and badly abused body.

"I'm sorry, Drake. I love you," she whispered. With that, the electricity was turned on again for what seemed like an eternity. When they turned it off, Drake's body continued to buck fiercely until the body stopped making a single sound. At first she thought he was dead but then Tiana heard low growling coming from his mouth.

"Wait! Stop!" Tiana yelled out just as they were about to turn the electricity on again. "I have some information about your son and your brother and your wife," Tiana screamed out. "You can kill me after, but let Drake go!"

S. Gates laughed again. "There is nothing you can tell me about my son and my brother except you that you decided you wanted to play with fire and kill them," he growled, getting close to her and grabbing a fistful of her hair.

"He wasn't your son," Tiana blurted out.

"What?" S. Gates hissed.

"In my bag there's a disc. Teema, she was fucking him and the baby was his," Tiana told him.

S. Gates released his grasp on her hair with a shove. She fell forward and hit her face on the concrete floor. It sent a bolt of pain through Tiana's entire body. She got up onto her knees and fell back down from her legs being so weak. Tiana refused to stay down. She was not about to give up. She pushed herself up again.

"Your brother was raping patients at the ward. And Teema was helping him. She participated in the rapes. He hated you and she said she only married you because she had to," Tiana said, still struggling to get to her feet.

"What the fuck are you talking about?" S. Gates snarled, his nostrils flaring. He could feel the gazes of his men baring down on him.

"Your wife, Teema Gates, who worked at the hospital under Teema Chambers, was fucking your brother and they had a baby. The boy wasn't yours anyway. They were planning on doing your ass dirty and running away together. All of the proof you need are on the discs in my bag," Tiana growled. She got to her feet. She swayed unsteadily, but at least she was able to look him in the eyes.

Within ten minutes, Blaine had a laptop with the discs playing in front of S. Gates. They were alone. S. Gates had swallowed hard more than once as he watched his wife and his brother perform ungodly acts on young girls. Then, he had cracked his knuckles over and over when he heard his wife admitting that she never loved him and saw the sight of his half brother fucking her brains out in his office. But, it was listening to her say over and over again that Silam Gates Jr. wasn't his son that sent S. Gates over the top.

"Argh!" he howled, sending the computer crashing to the floor. His chest rose and fell like a wild animal's. "Go get my wife and bring her to me," S. Gates said.

Blaine looked at him sympathetically. "Boss, um, maybe you should calm—" Blaine started.

"Bring her to me now!" he roared so loud Blaine had to plug his left ear with his pointer finger to keep it from ringing.

"What about the girl? What do you want us to do with her?" Blaine asked.

"Don't worry about her right now. Just go get me my wife," S. Gates said, calmly now. Blaine rushed out of the room without saying another word.

Once Gates was left alone to himself, he began kicking over chairs and tables, and roaring loudly. He was a man possessed. He had been crossed in the ultimate way and he was going to stop at nothing until his anger was satisfied.

"Please, Silam, you have to believe me. This girl is lying," Teema begged. She still looked beautiful and completely put together with not one hair out of place.

Tiana eyed Teema's perfectly coiffed hair, her expertly applied makeup, and the huge, sparkly canary diamond shining on her finger. *She didn't even need to work at Rollins. She has everything, which means she just did it to be a sick, twisted, nasty bitch.*

"I have the proof, you lying bitch!" Gates barked. He rushed over and slapped Teema across her face so hard, blood and spit shot from her mouth.

"Agh! Silam! Please!" she screamed. Teema knew all too well how abusive he could be when he was angry. She'd taken more than one ass whooping from him over the years.

Tiana smirked. She loved seeing Teema in pain. Even if he killed her after this, Tiana was ready to die now that she knew everyone who had wronged her was dead. She was going to die in peace.

"He was my half brother, you disloyal bitch. You told me you wanted to work there just so you could get out of the house. The whole time you were fucking him. You fucking piece-of-shit liar!" Gates spat.

Teema hung her head and sobbed. She knew there was no way out of this so she figured she might as well just tell the truth. "I never loved you! I hated my father for forcing me to marry you! He forced me so he could stay in your father's good graces in the drug business! I never wanted a man like you, like my own father!" Teema screamed cruelly.

As Tiana stood there she started to feel sorry for Teema. *No! This bitch did some disgusting things to us,* Tiana reminded herself.

"Kill her," Gates yelled at Blaine. "Kill her!" His voice rose.

"Please, Silam, don't do this. We both made mistakes. Let's just forget about all of this and move on together," Teema begged.

Blaine walked over to Teema and put his gun to her head. Teema closed her eyes and took her last breath.

"Blaine, wait." Silam put his hand up. "I have a better idea," he said as he walked over and took the gun out of Blaine's hand.

"Oh, thank God," Teema said, sounding relieved.

"Tiana!" he said as he walked over toward her and placed Blaine's gun in her hand. "You kill her."

"What?" Teema said with the same scared expression back on her face as she looked back and forth between Tiana, Silam, and Blaine.

Tiana gripped the gun in her hand and pointed it right at Teema. She couldn't keep her hands from shaking.

"Kill her now!" Gates screamed again. He rushed into Tiana like a bulldozer. Startled, Tiana stumbled a little bit.

"First, tell me why you didn't kill me at the club. Or at the headstone place. Or when I went away with you," Tiana said.

Gates looked at her pitifully. He shook his head from left to right.

"Why didn't you kill me all those times you had the opportunity to? You could have just killed me and moved on."

"Because I wanted to fuck with your head first. I wanted to make sure you saw your godmother and best friend

die. I wanted to make you suffer," he said with fury and
hatred in his voice. "Now kill her before I kill you," S.
Gates whispered. He was trying to hold on to his composure. He lifted his gun and leveled it at Tiana.

Tiana leveled her gun at Teema.

"Please! I'm begging—" Teema started.

Bam! Bam! Two bullets to the temple silenced her.
Then, within the blink of a second, she fired the gun
again. Bam! Bam! Bam! Silam's body fell to the floor with
two bullets to the chest and smack in the middle of his
head. Blaine tried to run to Silam and pry the gun from
his dead hand but Tiana shot him down before he could
get to it.

Tiana dropped the gun and fell to her knees. It was all
over now. She had survived and was still alive to tell the
story. She knew her father and godmother would have
been proud of her.

"Tiana," she heard her friend calling from a distance.

"Oh my God, Drake!" she yelled as she ran toward
him. Drake could barely move and he was drooling and
bleeding from his mouth. She could smell his burned
flesh and she couldn't believe he was still alive.

"Drake, hold on! You're going to be okay!" she reassured him as she knelt down beside him.

"Tiana," he said again as he struggled to breath.

"Yes, I'm here, Drake. Just hold on. You have to stay
awake, Drake," Tiana said as she took him into her arms.

"Tiana," he said as he looked up at her. "I love yo . . ."
Before he could get the last word out, his eyes rolled to
the back of his head and he took his last breath.

"Drake! No! You can't leave me!" Tiana cried out.
"Don't you fucking die on me! Wake up!" she screamed
as she pounded her fists onto his chest. "Wake up!
Wake up!" she kept saying as she rocked his body back
and forth.

William P. Rollins Psychiatric Hospital
Detroit, Michigan

"Wake up! Tiana! Wake up!" Celeste cried.

"She looks dead!" Izzy said in a panic.

"Tiana! Wake up! Please wake up!" Celeste cried, and this time she gently shook Tiana's badly injured head.

"How could he do this to her and just dump her in here like this? She's unconscious," Izzy said, exasperated. "I want this motherfucker to die, I swear."

"We have to take turns sitting up and watching her until she wakes up," Celeste said. She grabbed Tiana's hand and gave it a soft squeeze. "Just make it through this, Tiana. You have to push through. We need you here. Just wake up and I swear we will get our revenge on this bastard Dr. Syed. We will figure out how to get the fuck out of here and blow his car up. We'll get all the stuff so you can build a bomb. We'll do it just like you've always wanted. And then we will go after everyone in our lives who has ever hurt us, but you have to make it through this," Celeste spoke to Tiana softly.

She looked over at Izzy, who was sitting at the desk across from where Tiana lay. She was slumped over the desk with a pen and a legal notepad. Celeste looked over at Izzy like she was crazy.

"Our friend is in a fucking coma with no way to get her real help and you're writing a story?" Celeste snapped.

"What else do you expect me to do?" Izzy asked as she looked up at her roommate.

"I don't know, talk to her, tell her something that might get her to wake up."

"Oh, you mean you want me sit there and tell her lies like what you're doing right now?" Izzy asked.

"I don't know what you're talking about. I'm not lying to her," Celeste said, getting defensive.

"Yes, you are. You're sitting there telling her we're going to do all this shit that we're not ever gonna do in real life. You and I both know we're not getting out of here and killing anybody," Elizabeth said.

Celeste stayed quiet and looked down at her hands. "Call me a liar or whatever you want, but right now I'll say anything to her if it might get her to wake up."

"Look, Celeste, the reality is there's nothing we can do about any of this right now," Elizabeth said evenly. "We can complain, scream, and talk all the shit we want, but you and I both know they are not going to come and help her or us. If anything, they're gonna come and pump us with drugs if we start flipping out, so we might as well just sit quietly and hope and pray that she wakes up," Elizabeth said as she went back to writing whatever it was that she was writing.

"Fuck!" she yelled out as she grabbed the book and threw it to ground. "I'm scared, Cee Cee. What if this time she doesn't wake up?" she asked as the tears streamed down her face.

"She will fucking wake up," Celeste said with feeling. "She will wake up!"

Celeste and Elizabeth were forced out of their rooms four times before Tiana awoke. Celeste had just been returned from a "session" with Dr. Syed when she walked into the room and saw Tiana sitting up in her bed.

"Tiana! You're awake." Celeste rushed over to her excitedly.

Tiana parted a small smile.

"You have no idea how happy I am to see you up. What have you been dreaming about this whole time? That must've been some fucking awesome dream. I thought you would never come out of it," Celeste asked and answered all in one breath.

"He has to die," was the first thing that came out of Tiana's mouth.

"Who? What? How?" Celeste asked, her face folded into a deep frown.

"Dr. Syed. All of them will die. We will kill them all," Tiana said with confidence.

"Listen, your ass been out of it for days. I know we always talk about it, but c'mon, Tiana." Celeste smiled. "You know there's nothing we can do. We're stuck in this ward until they decide to let us back out into the real world."

"I'm serious, though! I know how to get us out of here," Tiana said to her. "It all came to me in a dream. It was a fucked-up dream because you and Izzy both died in it, but the beauty of it is we can change all of that." Tiana looked over at her friend who just stared blankly at her and didn't say a word. She knew she sounded a little bit crazy, but she didn't care.

"It was all a dream, Celeste; but, trust me, one day it will be a reality. I am going to make sure of that," Tiana vowed.